I0597525

NIGHT SOUNDS

A CHACE HAIG NOVEL

BLAZE WARD

Night Sounds
A Chace Haig Mission
Blaze Ward
Copyright © 2025 Blaze Ward
All rights reserved
Published by Knotted Road Press
www.KnottedRoadPress.com

ISBN: 978-1-64470-448-6

Cover art:
ID 30830624 © Captblack76 | Dreamstime.com

Cover and interior design copyright © 2025 Knotted Road Press

Never miss a release!
If you'd like to be notified of new releases, sign up for my newsletter.

http://www.blazeward.com/newsletter/

Buy More!
Did you know that you can buy directly from the Knotted Road Press website?

https://www.knottedroadpress.com/shop/

This book is licensed for your personal enjoyment only. All rights reserved. This is a work of fiction. All characters and events portrayed in this book are fictional, and any resemblance to real people or incidents is purely coincidental. This book, or parts thereof, may not be reproduced in any form without permission.

NO AI TRAINING: Without in any way limiting the author's [and publisher's] exclusive rights under copyright, any use of this publication to "train" generative artificial intelligence (AI) technologies to generate text is expressly prohibited. The author reserves all rights to license uses of this work for generative AI training and development of machine learning language models.

ALSO BY BLAZE WARD

The Science Officer Series

Start with: The Science Officer

The Jessica Keller Chronicles

Start with: Auberon

CS-405 (Command Centurion Kosnett, part of Jessica)

Start with: Queen Anne's Revenge

First Centurion Kosnett (sequel to Jessica)

Start with: Encounter at Vilahana

Additional Alexandria Station Stories

Alexandria Station Collection

Handsome Rob (Alexandria Station Universe)

Start with: Can't Shoot Straight Gang

=====================

Corsac Fox

Start with: Flight of the Corsac Fox

Operation Marrakesh

Start with: Trial by Leviathan

Captain Daring

Start with: Revoked

The Hunter Bureau

Start with: Mirrors

Fairchild

Chace Haig had studied the sidewalk and walkway carefully for ten minutes before approaching. Listened to the night sounds. Watched foot traffic with extra care from both the front seat of his borrowed car before and then as he walked a pair of squares around the block, larger first and then smaller as he zeroed in.

Nothing stood out from the pattern of Seattle's darkness. Not that he knew the city all that well, but he'd spent enough time here on various missions over the last few years.

Capital Hill, where the city's old money lived, with the tech newcomers across the lake in their palaces. Not physically all that close to the old Chinatown now called the International District, but emotionally close, even as the Vietnamese had largely moved in as the old Cantonese money had traded up the social ladder. Rather like how the Italians had replaced the Irish in Manhattan, back in the day.

Lots of money, though most of it was legitimate in Seattle. Still a lot of underworld folks looking for ways to launder things. To get their kids into those elite schools. To hobnob with the tech millionaires and billionaires that made up a distinct geological layer of the city's culture.

Sometimes, things still went wrong in this business. Chace touched the inside of his left arm to the SIG Sauer P365, under his jacket. The SIG Anti-Snag (SAS) 9mm, loaded with special ammunition by Weland, his armorer back in DC. That woman had a meanness about her professionalism that Chace appreciated. Jacketed softnose rounds with a sliver of hardened steel like a nail down the center. Open up like a drill bit on a normal person. Punch a tiny hole through any armor but a titanium plate over the heart, which was why he'd been trained to fire a little high or a little low, depending.

If he had to shoot someone, he wanted them staying down. Hopefully, nothing like that was necessary tonight.

He stirred and moved finally, detaching from the nearby shadows and starting his final approach. There was a silencer for his SIG, but screwing it on right now showed premeditation. If he got into trouble, he'd toss it down the sewer before the cops arrived.

Assuming the trouble could be contained. He had two spare magazines in his pocket to go with the one on his shoulder rig. If thirty-one rounds wasn't enough, he had other troubles.

Not that he looked like trouble. Nice charcoal chinos. Blue button-down shirt. Black wool blazer that looked casual. Like he was the banker he ascribed to being the real world.

At least with folks that didn't know what he really did for a living. Any of his livings.

Chace breathed deep and calm, meditating in motion as he came up the front steps of the old craftsman house. The porch light was off, by design. The inside lights were off, as well. At least the ground floor. There was a bedroom lit above, but those had been his instructions.

He rapped quietly on the glass storm door and waited, turning sideways enough to keep an eye on the street. Side street. Quiet neighborhood. Capital Hill. Seattle.

Where darker things might lurk out of sight.

The pause was long enough that his hand twitched ever so slightly towards his SIG, but Chace controlled the motion with the same discipline he mastered his breathing.

Finally, the bolt opened. Then the door moved a crack. There was a darker shadow, peeking through where a chain might stop the average person from kicking the door in.

He turned enough for her to see his face and nodded.

"Haig," he said with just enough voice that she could hear it.

The door closed again and he heard her pulling the chain open. It opened again a moment later and Chace had a chance to study the woman.

Xi Xiao-He. Hong Kong born Cantonese. Born the same year the Soviet Union collapsed. Watched the People's Republic reclaim the ancient territory when she was six. Parents had gotten out on British passports, though he hadn't dug too deep there, with the family eventually ending up in Vancouver, BC.

Small woman. Wiry, from the pictures he'd seen. Face reminded him of a young Michelle Yeoh, from her martial arts action movies in the 80s. Long, black hair pulled back.

"Ready?" he asked quietly, watching her for signs.

And keeping track of the darkness behind her inside, in case this was a trap and he had to talk or shoot his way out. Wouldn't be the first time, but she'd called him for help.

"I am," she replied, crisp English tones like the BBC World Service.

He moved a step to one side and nodded. She grabbed a duffel bag from beside the door and shouldered it before reaching for the storm door and opening it.

He'd instructed her to dress in dark colors, without any visible jewelry. It was nice to see that she'd listened as she joined him on the porch.

"Last chance to change your mind," he said simply.

"If I stay, it's only a matter of time until he gets drunk and hits me," she snarled in a quiet, British tone. "Or kills me and pays a blood fee, even if they kill him for it. I'd rather be free."

Chace nodded. He appreciated her quandary.

Arranged marriage, as was common with the old Cantonese culture. Doubly so, as she'd come from money originally, though it had fallen on harder times by the time she'd gotten out of college. Married off to one of the Chinese crime families that had been here almost as long as Seattle had.

Chace didn't know Jun Tie-Yong except by reputation. And the reports the Institute had been able to quietly borrow from the FBI and a few other agencies. Xiao-He's about-to-be-former husband was a mid-level manager on one of the nastier tongs around here. Benevolent Societies on the surface, taking care of Chinese immigrants in an earlier era where the white settlers had hated them almost as much as they had blacks or natives.

Not a lot had changed in Seattle today, save that a lot of South Asians had come with the various tech booms later and been slotted into the mix as well.

Chace went ahead and drew his pistol, holding it down by his side as he turned and nodded her to follow. He's left the car down a block and change. The Institute had provided it once they had determined that this was a good use of Chace as an agent.

On paper, Chace worked for Mueller Investments of Zurich as a banker. If you had a need, you called Chace, and he'd hook you up with someone, somewhere, legality not necessarily mattering.

In reality, his technical employer was the International Legal Research Institute, itself a quiet and almost forgotten organization most recently attached to the US Department of Treasury, though it had originally been a CIA/FBI/MI5/MI6 Joint Service Intelligence Strike Operation that allowed arm's length plausible deniability when it ran deep cover agents into the global criminal underworld.

The first Chace Haig had been active in the 1960s. He was the sixth man to assume the identity. And the job.

If you had a need, you called Chace Haig, and he knew a guy...

Tonight, he was rescuing a princess from a dragon's tower. That was how his boss had described it, after the original request had come in through one of the email channels he supposedly maintained and been vetted.

He made it to the sidewalk and turned right, head on a swivel and not offering to help Xiao-He with her bag. The night sounds hadn't changed, and she moved almost as silently as he did.

Down the block. Across the intersection. Chace had parked on this side, facing away, to make it easy. Every step planned, especially when doing something like this.

His free hand found the remote fob in his blazer pocket as they got close and Chace popped the trunk. Custom Audi A4 sedan in muted burgundy. The sort of thing a banker should drive, because you wanted sedate and responsible when handing someone a lot of money to invest.

Ferraris were a warning signal in this business. Most businesses.

The trunk popped open, a maw of darkness because he'd turned off the light inside with one of Weland's custom switches. Just as she handled guns personally, the woman oversaw an entire department that handled other gear for him. This car was almost an exact copy of her current one, save that Chace hadn't lost his legs just above the knees in a car bombing in Iraq like she had.

"Open your bag and dump the contents in," he ordered her. "Then toss the bag into the gutter."

She looked at him blankly for a moment, then recognition nodded. Someone might be tracking her and suitcases and bags were the easiest way to hide such things.

He reached into his jacket pocket now and pulled out a small sniffer device that he pointed at the bag as she worked.

Sure enough, it was broadcasting a signal. Almost like those things you could put on your phone of your earbuds if you lost something. Might be one, sewn into a seam or something.

He didn't care enough to locate it and smash it at this point. Instead, he watched the little arrow point as the bag got dropped.

"What is that?" she asked, standing with both arms wrapped around herself like she was cold, even though it was a warm spring night.

He pointed it at her and found a second signal, right in line with the center of her chest.

"You're broadcasting a tracking signal," he told her, tilting the device down to show it.

She looked down, still blank.

"Take off your bra inside your shirt and put it with the bag," he ordered.

Grumbles this time, but she complied, withdrawing one arm and then the other from her sleeves and doing that particular magic trick all women learned at some point.

The signal followed the bra into the gutter.

He scanned her again, just to be sure, but her shoes were clean. That was the other place that was commonly used, since you could open up the heel and slip something in without it being obvious.

A quick scan of the trunk revealed nothing, so if there were any others, they were turned off until someone activated them with a signal.

Hopefully, Weland's electronics in the car would see them at that moment.

Chace's head suddenly came up.

There is a scent to danger. Chace's various instructors had pounded that into him over the years, as they took the boy he'd once been and turned him into a secret agent, before eventually graduating him to the role of Chace Haig himself.

Those night sounds had changed.

He smelled trouble. There wasn't any other way to describe it. His head came around as headlights pulled out from two blocks up, another low profile sedan rolling down the hill slowly, like folks reading house numbers for a place they didn't know. Or looking for parking, because there was never enough on Cap Hill. Except that they'd been parked ten seconds ago.

Chace tossed the scanner into the trunk and slammed it in a single motion. His off-hand found the fob and unlocked the doors.

"In," he snapped sharply, moving to the passenger side and pulling the door open. It took her a moment, so Chace grabbed Xiao-He and pulled her, thrusting her to safety and closing the door, because he understood the level of armor protection this sedan had.

The other car rolled closer, passenger window down because it was the sole dark spot where the other windows reflected street lights.

A hand emerged from the passenger side holding something dark as it started to come alongside. Chace didn't wait to identify it at all, dropping to a half-squat behind the trunk and putting his first two shots into the darkness of the car.

A single shot came back. Well, up, fired into the sky when the passenger took at least one bullet north of the collarbones. Chace put another pair of shots where he could see the driver backlit, even as the vehicle began to speed up.

It lost control and plowed into the third car in front of the Audi, horn blaring because the driver had collapsed against it, then silence a moment later as all the airbags deployed in a huge pop of noise.

Chace wasn't waiting to see what happened next. He went around the Audi and opened the door, sliding in in a single motion. The vehicle didn't need a key inserted, as he could remote start it at the same time he opened the locks, so it was already purring.

Xiao-He already had her seatbelt on by the time he joined her, measuring the gap in front of him and doing the geometry for what was probably a fourteen point turn reversing.

All those tactical driving classes came to the fore as he dropped the car into gear and pulled delicately into the narrow street. Ahead of him, another pair of lights approaching slowly.

Something wasn't right. He slammed the car into reverse and reached out with his mind to find all the parked cars closing in on both sides.

The approaching car had stopped. Even as he watched both directions, he saw the passenger door open and suddenly bullets slammed into his windshield.

Probably would have gone through a normal car. There was a reason he hadn't picked up a rental for this job. They'd need something heavier to threaten him.

Xiao-He screamed once, then caught herself and turned perfectly silent. Chace had an arm across the back of her seat and his head back as he accelerated away. More bullets, but nothing on this car was at risk of a 9mm or whatever they were using. Just more lead to wax off later.

After he got away.

Chace hit the top of the little hill with times screaming and snapped the car to something like a reverse bootlegger reverse at the intersection, trusting that nobody was driving on the side street and the gunfire hadn't attracted any pedestrians who were too dark to see before he hit them.

There was no way in hell he was stopping to render assistance tonight.

"They've backed up," Xiao-He said in a tight, controlled voice.

"Circling around to come after us," Chace replied. "I might have missed a transmitter somewhere and don't have time to look. Hold on and let me know if you have to throw up. There are bags in the glove compartment."

"Why do you—no, drive," she began.

Chace slammed the Audi into motion and rolled. There were really only a handful of ways to get off Capital Hill in Seattle. He'd memorized them a while ago, and drove them whenever he was in town, because most of his clientele in Seattle proper tended to be up here.

North took him to the bridges, pinched in by Lake Union and Lake Washington. West was down to downtown and I-5, with quick access to I-90 if the traffic wasn't utterly stupid on Madison at this time of night. Which it probably was.

He hit 15th and headed south. Options to Broadway and doubling back if he needed, up onto 90 itself to cross Lake Washington, or bomb down Rainier and come out near the Boeing factory in Renton in a while.

At Madison, he smelled them, a pair of headlights back there that didn't feel right and were closing faster than this neighborhood preferred. Chace got lucky on the light and turned right instead of getting stuck behind some Vegan yuppie in a hybrid on their way to the Coop market. Traffic was heavier, but that was folks headed down into town.

Behind him, headlights marked that other sedan.

Chace took a moment to locate the controls he needed. The car's entertainment unit wasn't even remotely similar to what had come from the factory, but Weland had added all sorts of goodies that weren't accessible unless the fob was within 4 meters of the sensor.

"What is that?" Xiao-He asked in a quiet voice, in case he needed to ignore her while slaloming through slower traffic like a foot at night. Not the only one, from the cherry red mustang that suddenly saw this as a challenge. Or a game.

Chace kept one hand on the wheel and dialed buttons from memory.

"Jammer system," he replied. "Normally good for all sorts of things. Right now, I want whatever bug they are following to be overwhelmed."

"Why is he doing this?" she asked.

Chace assumed he was her soon to be ex-husband, assuming Chace could outdrive a pair of yahoos in the other sedan.

And the fool in the arrest-me-red mustang roaring up on his ass as Chace slowed, then blasted into a left turn through a gap in oncoming traffic that had Xiao-He gasp just short of another scream.

He focused on the street. Narrower here and reconstructed recently to the point that the intersection ahead was slightly offset.

That silly shit in the mustang had turned as well, but the other sedan had been caught.

They tried to run the light anyway and Chace watched them get broadsided by a flatbed truck that usually meant Mexican lawn professionals.

He sighed a bit of relief that he could probably get away, then that jackass in the mustang came right up on his ass and overrevved his engine loud enough that Chace heard it.

Really?

He understood what kind of guy drove a red mustang in this town. And from the sound, it wasn't even something impressive like an SVT Cobra. Or at least a GT.

No, fool was running around in an LS with glass packs.

What a friend of Chace's usually called the *Pussy Mustang*.

Chace slowed down enough to annoy the fucker, wondering if the guy was somehow a deep cover op for Jun Tie-Yong, tracking the car for the others.

If so, his cell phone was dead right now, along with every other electronic device within fifty meters of the Audi until Chace dialed down the broadcast power.

As Weland and others had told him when dealing with certain situations, there was no extra credit for neatness.

He got to Rainier and turned left. Dipshit stayed right behind him until the light at Dearborn, then popped up on Chace's left and revved the hell out of those measly six cylinders like a chihuahua growling at at mastiff

Windows on both cars were smoked enough to be darkness both ways, but Chace was watching for a window to come down for another shooter.

Anything else he could deal with right now.

Just to be a shit, he dropped the car into neutral and revved back at the man. It had to be a man. Woman with that sort of attitude problem would be in an overdone Honda riceburner or a Porsche, depending on how much money she had.

"Seriously?" Xiao-He asked.

Chace smiled as she rolled her eyes at both of them.

"It might be a trap," he said. "And he might just be an asshole."

"You're going to race when the light changes?" she asked.

Chace dropped it into gear as it went green and took the accelerator to the floor. For all the armor protecting them, it still had a stupid amount of horsepower.

The tires screamed as the car generated g-forces sufficient to press both of them into the seats.

The mustang was lost in a haze of smoke.

He backed off after making his point. The dipshit apparently wanted a second try, because he came up on the left again as Chace counted down the meters.

At the last possible moment, Chace snapped the wheel over, cutting across the car in the turn lane and hitting the curving onramp to eastbound 90 at a speed unsafe for most drivers.

There was nobody in front of him or behind him, so he was doing around ninety when he emerged from the far side of the tunnel. Chase went ahead and backed it down to the flow of traffic as he entered the tunnel and slid in with everyone crossing the bridge.

Inside, he cut the jammer and turned on a different scanner, but nothing was broadcasting that he could detect. Considering who had built the car, that meant he was safe.

They hit the floating bridge and Chace settled into the middle lane.

"Now, you should be safe," he said. "Sorry about your bag, but I have spare in the trunk and I'll scan everything again when I let you out. How are you doing?"

"I'm going to need to use a restroom at some point," she announced in that BBC journalist tone. "Possibly some coffee to calm my nerves. How soon until we get where we're going?"

"I've arranged a safehouse in Issaquah for you," he said. "Folks I've worked with before and trust. They'll hide you for a couple of days, until your husband's people assume that you've made it out of town. Presumably, they will shift their focus to BC at that point, so you'll have a different passport and drivers license when you get on the plane to Boston. Given the number of folks like your husband there, I'd recommend someplace safer, but you hired me to get you this far, and make the arrangements to get you there."

"And I appreciate it," she said. "I have friends and family in Boston who will hide me for a time, then protect me from Tie-Yong when I divorce him. If that fails, I might call you again, but I have a lot of money stashed in safe places."

"If that fails, likely your estate will need to be settled in probate court," he told her. "Tie-Yong and his ilk play rough. You shouldn't ever stop looking over your shoulder if you stay in country. Honestly, London's probably safer for you with the new passport you have."

"London?" she asked, surprised and intrigued.

"Mostly Russian and Central Asian types," he nodded. "The old Hong Kong money that got out, like yours is generally legitimate by now. I can even introduce you to some people if you need."

She laughed.

"Chace Haig, the man to call when you need something done," she said. "Or need an introduction. Or shooting people?"

"Occupational hazard," he shrugged as they climbed out at Factoria. "Nobody there is likely to want to press charges, so it will go unsolved."

"How can you be so certain?" she pressed.

"Because they don't want sunlight," he smiled ferally.

She flinched under his gaze and his tone, which he'd intended. Her tone had gotten flirtatious, and the last thing he needed was a fling with a client. Even a beautiful one about to be single.

Chace concentrated on his driving as she got quiet.

He'd get her to safety, then check in with his boss and see if they needed to move aggressively to crush Jun Tie-Yong and his segment of the tongs in Seattle.

Or merely let them get away.

For now.

Chace walked into the diner and located his next target, seated in a quiet booth a little away from the few other nightbirds out too late. Out of Seattle and home on the East Coast. Whatever home was.

He watched the woman as he approached.

Thane Avison. His boss, both on paper and in real life. Middle-aged black woman. One of the first field agents originally hired when the FBI let black women carry guns. Thirty-odd years later the hair was gray and in short locs today. She wore a similar outfit to his, but a little more formal.

Old enough to be his mother, so he didn't know what the waitress would think of them meeting like this. Didn't really care.

She studied him as he crossed the space and slid into the booth across from her. The waitress was there with coffee, but got sent back for decaf.

Chace's sleep was messed up enough as it was. He didn't need to see the sunrise this morning, unless Thane had another mission for him.

"You look like hell," she said quietly as they were alone again.

He picked up the menu and considered some food rather than answering.

"How are you holding up?" she asked when he didn't speak.

Chace shrugged. He was a deep-cover secret agent on the fringes of the underworld, meeting and introducing strangers to other folks for a finder's fee, most of the time. The Institute had an amazing file of such names, numbers, and contact information, and his memory was close enough to photographic, most of the time.

"It is what it is," he finally said when it was clear she would outwait him.

"I read the report," she continued with a sly smile. "That silly mustang driver wasn't anybody that mattered, but we went ahead and inserted a couple of fun tickets into his record, next time the police or insurance company runs them."

Chace nodded. Everything being electronic meant that systems could be adjusted, leaving people none the wiser. Rude to reach back and slap the guy after he'd lost his little exhibition of machismo, but Chace was just the agent.

"Any calls come in?" he asked.

Most of the time, his ringer was off and folks knew to leave a voice mail with enough pertinent information. Or to deliver cryptic emails to one of a handful of accounts, where his service would route them forward.

That his service also happened to be directly connected to various acronym agencies in Virginia and a few other places never came up on polite conversation.

"The usual," she replied, allowing herself to be deflected for the moment. "Nothing that you need to worry about. Two or three we've gone ahead and handled *sub rosa* for you, so you can check the reports when you get back."

"Get back?" he asked, head coming up from picking which salad he'd order.

Chace Haig was tall and slender, with wiry muscles. The original had been that way, and the trainers had selected for build and genetics in replacing him each time. It also required an iron discipline when eating, because food today had so many ugly fillers and corn syrup when you were in the States.

Just one of many reasons he preferred London or Paris.

"The folks reading the report suggest that you've maintained a high operational tempo for too long," Thane nodded, keeping her tones so quiet that the next booth would miss them. "That you need some downtime to release stress. I can't let you go be that other guy, but I want you to take two or three weeks and not answer your phone for anybody but me calling. File a report, but pick a place and disappear into vacation mode. And that's an official order, in case you felt like arguing with me."

Chace let go the breath, words unspoken, and nodded. Probably not the worst idea. Racing that idiot in the mustang had been a spur of the moment thing, but it had also been a severe break in his professionalism, even if there had been an outside chance that the man was working for someone.

There are only necessary actions, and mistakes.

That had not be necessary.

"Do you care where?" he asked, rolling through a variety of climates and cultures in his head.

"Not really," she said. "No, strike that. Stay out of Switzerland. I don't want you popping into the office in Zurich for any reason. You need a break. A vacation, though I am aware that you haven't really been off duty in almost two years. Take the time and see what you need."

"Yes, mother," he grinned.

She matched it. Thane never talked about her personal life, so he had no idea if she had a husband. Or a wife. Or kids. Or anything.

She was his boss, but also his confessor. And occasionally his other mother, his own family nobody that he ever talked to. That other fellow had been supposedly killed in a car wreck, just after college, allowing him to make a clean break.

And eventually turn into Chace Haig.

The waitress returned with the orange pot and got their orders as Chace considered where he might go, if nobody was needing anything from him.

Chace didn't like to think of himself as shallow, but part of this job benefited from an extroverted personality that didn't go in for introspection much.

After all, he lied to everyone for a living. Except Thane.

Connected criminals with other criminals for a fee, filing occasional reports that let various law enforcement agencies all over the world update their records and plan those big jobs where dozens of folks get arrested all at once.

But he didn't really exist. Or rather, he'd inherited a set of tendencies that the original Chace Haig had established nearly sixty years ago, only slowly adapting forward as cultures evolved.

Jazz, because the original hadn't really been into rock and roll. Certain drinks. Certain foods. Certain sartorial choices that had at least modernized. Still, not all that removed from what they'd been then.

But who was he today?

The face in the mirror was a stranger this morning. All the plastic surgery had planed him down and turned him into someone else, but Chace saw that other guy looking out from those brown eyes today.

Chace shrugged commiseratingly to him and finished brushing his teeth.

He'd initially considered going to London, because it was one of his favorite cities, but then that quiet voice in the back of his head had reminded him that he'd run into folks he knew, everywhere he went, and would get drawn back into work regardless.

So he hadn't quite tossed a dart at a map, but still ended up in Tokyo. But one of the modern, nicer places that catered to Westerners who weren't prepared for the whole Nihon cultural immersion thing.

Chace was vaguely passable in Japanese, but not even remotely conversational. Much of the time he operated out of the States or Western Europe.

Yet one more reason to be as far away from that as he could get, and hadn't wanted to winter in Australia or New Zealand.

Dressed like a western business tourist this morning, he took himself down to a breakfast as a Frenchman might have done such a thing, rather than the American he was. Croissant with excessive butter and some jam options. Fresh fruit. A few dried meat cuts and some cheese.

And he was conversational in French. Less so in Quebecois, but that was almost a second language by accent and he didn't spend enough time in Montreal to polish things.

Late morning, because he'd taken a red eye via Paris to get here, spending basically a day and a half in the process.

First class upgrade points were vastly underrated by most travelers.

He could feel a layer of something peel like skin as he sat and listened to quiet music and sipped tea while munching. A few other business folk, possibly also recovering from long travels, shared the restaurant with him. Chace made a point to study faces surreptitiously, noting that one group looked Mainland Chinese.

Northerners, if he had to guess. Probably Taiwanese in town doing trade in technology, the East China Sea being something of a moat separating the People's Republic from the Western-oriented nations largely opposing communist aggression.

If you could still call them communists these days. Chace remembered a professor at Yale describe them as merely the latest dynasty, after the Yuan, the Ming, the Qing, and the Republic under the Kuomintang in the Warlord Era. And even then, the KMT might not qualify, if you looked at other periods of unrest surrounding the fall of any given dynasty.

Xi might merely be the latest Emperor of China, though Chace wasn't sure if the man would be insulted or honored at the comparison.

Not today's problem.

Instead, Chace let the morning pass uneventfully, eventually changing into swim trunks and spending some time by the pool, lounging in the shade and sipping the occasional sidecar.

More layers seemed to evaporate as he did, so Chace stopped grumbling at Thane's enforced downtime. Apparently, he really had needed it more than he'd imagined.

Mid-afternoon, it was a traditional cocktail hour, so Chace showered and put on his banker costume to attend, though without the tie because he wasn't *that kind* of banker.

Folks sipped various concoctions and munched on a buffet, mostly chatting with strangers.

It was one thing Chace had come to understand about such events. If it was a company party, everyone stayed in their department and office groups. At a mixer, however, everyone was busy hustling every stranger they could meet, uncertain which one might be the connection that made their quarter or their career.

He had brought an extra box of the nicer business cards with him to Japan. Just his name, an email address, and the bank, on the heaviest stock and embossed in gold.

Normally, you held it in both hands and bowed when delivering, but everyone had a drink, or had had several drinks, so things were a bit more flexible. And most of the folks in here weren't Japanese, so they took a more American approach.

"Banker?" one gentleman asked. "Mueller Investments of Zurich? What do they do?"

"Boutique investments for high-net-worth individuals," Chace nodded, his tone suggesting that nine figures was the minimum value for someone wanting his people to even take your calls.

That wasn't entirely true, because most of his real clients were worth far less, though possibly even more exclusive.

The man nodded, possibly disappointed.

"As they say in the business, if you have a need, I know a guy..." Chace continued, his normal business pitch.

Again, exclusive. Upper crust.

Or criminals just breaking out of the penny ante games and moving up, where they had money and needed a way to invest it without all those pesky rules and laws and financial disclosures.

For the longest time, it had been property in London and Vancouver, but US Treasury had finally started really leaning on the Brits and the Canadians on money laundering, and much of that had gone elsewhere, where it frequently had to now take several hops to be clean.

If a couple of major banks in Germany and Switzerland ever finally got caught with their hands in the cookie jar, then the game might get very interesting.

Chace captured this gentleman's card in turn. Shen Heng Ru. Industrialist, which was even more vague than banker. His associate was a slightly-younger man, perhaps forty, named Ren Ning Su, who appeared to be a sidekick more than anything, as he hardly spoke.

"And yourself?" Chace asked.

"Investments in various manufacturing concerns," Shen replied with equal evasiveness. "Japan is forever on the cutting edge of things, competing with Korea, and we want to stay up with them."

Chace nodded. That was pretty much the story of East Asia over the last fifty years. Perhaps longer in the case of Japan, Inc., but the opening of China under Deng Xiao-Ping had brought a billion workers into the global industrial economy, driving down prices for everything everywhere, even as it had continued to hollow out low-end manufacturing in the developed nations, as East and South Asia could do it cheaper.

Generally by outsourcing a type of work hardly better than slavery, but the Americans had put raw capitalists in charge of the government under Reagan and then let them get away with anything they wanted since.

Not that Chace had strong opinions on the topic. Nor the man he'd been in the old days.

"Perhaps we will be able to do business, sometime," Chace allowed, nodding to the two men as the tides of the room moved them one way and him the other.

He doubted it, but it was what he did.

And crime never slept.

Cai Yan-Li nodded as he listened to the man describe the latest mission. Surveillance, which was really what they were always after. Learn what their foes were doing so it could be stolen, adapted, or destroyed before it became a threat.

His office was kept dim, but that was a personal preference going back several decades. And today, he was feeling all of his sixty-three years.

Dark stained paneling on the two walls that weren't covered by book cases. A bonsai tree nearly three feet tall and ancient as they went. Desk done in the English style, because they had left such a deep cultural imprint on Hong Kong and much of the south that it was still there a generation after they had been finally forced out as the sun got serious about setting on their damnable empire.

"Wait, repeat that," Yan-Li snapped, dropping out of his reverie and voice locking hard. "What was his name again?"

"Chace Haig, sir," Heng-Ru repeated carefully. "I have his card with an email address at Mueller Investments of Zurich, Switzerland."

"Take a picture of the card and forward it as soon as we are off the call," Yan-Li ordered. "Describe the man."

Could it be? After...thirty-five years. Was that possible?

"American, sir," Heng-Ru began. "Mid-thirties, perhaps, with brown hair a little long for a Swiss banker and dressed more American business casual than a suit. Roughly one hundred and eighty-five centimeters tall, with a thin build. Seemed intelligent and I heard him address various others in several languages, often with a native accent."

Heng-Ru fell silent at that and Yan-Li let the man stew. Shen Heng-Ru was a low-level operative for the organization. A spy, but not anything useful. Just an investor representing other funds and money that might want to invest in your factory, if due diligence revealed anything worth stealing later.

"Sir?" Heng-Ru asked after a long pause.

"Fill out a complete report," Yan-Li ordered. "In greater detail than you would imagine, down to everything you can think of. Then do not engage the man again. Am I clear?"

"You are, sir," the agent replied. "We were only intending to be here for a few days. Should we move to a different hotel under some pretense?"

"Yes, immediately," Yan-Li acknowledged. "Remove yourself from the arena. Do it quietly, but effectively."

"Understood, sir," Heng-Ru said. "Is there anything else I should be doing?"

"No," Yan-Li said. "Your report is what I need as soon as it can be transmitted."

He hung up and spun his chair to gaze up at the portrait hanging above his desk and constantly looking down over his shoulder.

Cai Yong-Tao. *The Chairman* himself, who had, nearly two centuries ago, founded a small organization that had been dedicated to driving all the foreigners out of China. Hong Kong was almost the wedge to shatter the entirety of China in those days, but the British had been content to simply trade, and had even helped his ancestors weaken the Qing.

Later, the Harmonious Fists had risen up and attempted to drive out both, plus all the other Westerners, only be almost completely anni-hilated for their efforts.

Almost.

Today, Yan-Li studied his great-great-great-grandfather and nodded to the man's terrible, severe image, painted in traditional robes, despite his utter despisal of the Qing, those damnable foreigner Manchus.

Yan-Li meditated on the lessons that the Chairman had sent down the generations to the present. The rise of the Nationalists who had thrown down the Qing eventually. They had just ended up being Westerners with Chinese faces. The Maoists, who had been willing to accept support from Hong Kong tongs that had eventually succeeded in forcing the Manchu to flee to Taiwan and Japan, where a few were still being hunted today.

Or their descendants.

"Yes, Chairman Cai," he nodded to the great man's ghost. "I will see it done."

He turned back to his desk and dialed a number.

"Come here, immediately," he said when it stopped ringing, then hung up again and waited.

The door opened quietly and Chun-Bin entered. Number Two Daughter, but of all his children, she had been the one that had taken to the family business.

Not shipping. Her siblings had learned all those bits and were generally effective, save for the one artist who wanted merely enough inheritance to simply paint with his days. And had some measure of talent, from the news Yan-Li had quietly followed.

"Sir?" she asked, coming to attention.

"I have a mission for you," Yan-Li said simply. "It may be nothing but surveillance. It may be a fool's errand. And it may be serious."

She nodded, silent, and he studied her for a moment.

Educated at the University of Southern California, where she'd also studied a variety of other things that she would need later. Hong Kong born, Americanized to a certain extent, and tri-cultural when you considered the merchants of the south and the party fanatics of the north.

"There is a man," Yan-Li continued after a beat. "He is in Tokyo right now. You will locate him, identify him, and then stand by for more orders."

She nodded again. Some of the folks he had sent her to train under had left Hong Kong with the British, a few ending up in Hollywood because they didn't trust the Party.

Yan-Li didn't trust the Party, but he owned enough of the right people to have warning whenever trouble was brewing. Nor was he foolish enough to challenge the cadres in any public way, having watched more than one of the supposed Chinese Billionaires be brought to heel with a snap of Beijing's chains.

"Does he have a name?" Chun-Bin asked in a somber tone.

"Chace Haig," Yan-Li told his daughter. "American. Possibly a spy, but I cannot be certain."

"Sir?"

Confusion. To be expected.

"I once tangled with an American spy named Chace Haig," Yan-Li continued. "Like this one, he claimed to be a Swiss banker. It may be entirely coincidental. Or perhaps a relative, as your target is far too young to be the man in question. Even the chance, however, must be investigated, and, if necessary, eliminated."

She nodded.

"This is personal, Chun-Bin," he told her, watching her face grow even more serious. "In 1988, he shot me, right here."

A hand found the spot in his left shoulder where the bullet had somehow missed anything important by no more than it's width, letting that Haig go on to stop an operation that might have unraveled Deng's effort to fully open China to the West.

And all the troubles that had come with it.

"I failed," he told her. "There is a report you will read and memorize. We could have stopped things in 1988. Failing that, we have had to work hard to build up the Party and the mainland since then, into a thing that could repulse another wave of colonization, however much money flowed in. The Americans and British have never forgiven the Party for 1949, and seek every opportunity to undo what Mao achieved that they could let those brutal bastards of the KMT return. That cannot be allowed."

"And if he is somehow connected with those people?" she asked.

"Then we will kill him," Yan-Li nodded. "Go, and prepare to go under cover after my nemesis, if he somehow turns out to be such a thing."

She bowed and left him alone. Yan-Li found himself touching that old wound, and remembering all the failures that had come of it.

This could not be the same man, as the Chace Haig knew had dueled with would also be in his sixties now. But Yan-Li had several children, and one that would possibly ascend to the Chaimanship herself one of these days when he was done.

Perhaps if this was another American spy, and she could ride the glory of killing him to the point that Yan-Li could begin to retire soon and turn things over to her.

He would not fail again.

CHAPTER
FIVE

Chace almost felt like a new man after five days of resort living. He'd left the grounds a few times, but never gone any deeper into Tokyo than the tourist areas, where he didn't mind being desperately overcharged for things. Tokyo was an expensive city, but it made up for it with the depth of possibilities.

Not his normal field of operations, though, and he didn't feel like expanding. Thane had similar deep cover agents in East Asia that did the same sorts of things Chace Haig did. And looked like natives in any crowd, where he stood out for being tall and white.

He did understand, however, how to be Japanese polite, and that got him a lot of mileage with folks, so his shopping trips went easy and he had money to spend on little things that caught his eye.

Another cocktail party. He hadn't gone every afternoon, but had at least drifted through briefly. The crowd was largely changed today, because the weekend was coming and folks had headed home while others had come in a little early to have some free time before Monday morning.

Chace had a sidecar in one hand and a loose, vacuous smile on his face. Bankers weren't supposed to be the center of attention, so he handed out his card, gave brief and evasive explanations, then moved on to listening to other folks impress him with whatever lies they wished to peddle.

Most of these folks even seemed perfectly legitimate, but he wasn't scouting. If someone contacted him later, they would open themselves up to whatever the CIA and other agencies wanted to get roped in by Thane.

Tomorrow's problem. He found himself studying the woman as she walked across the room. She had a magnetism that drew everyone's eye, so he didn't feel bad for staring at her.

Chinese. Possibly Cantonese, but he'd have to be closer to actually tell. Medium height, athletic build that showed lean muscles he generally associated with dancers or martial artists. Black hair a little long and styled up with a pair of chopsticks holding it.

She moved like a predator. Most of the businessmen in here reacted like prey. He wasn't surprised when they ended up orbiting one another. Most of the faces around them were bit players on stage to make the scene, rather than main actors advancing the plot, once he'd met them.

Chace smiled. She returned it.

"Chace Haig," he introduced himself, glass in one hand and cautious eye watching the crowd around them watch back.

He supposed that the age gaps here might have played a factor. Chace was in his mid-thirties now. This woman looked to be late twenties, plus or minus as much as a decade, given how some Chinese women aged. The rest of the crowd started at forty and went north quickly.

"Rowena Cai," she said, watching him like the name would mean something, but it didn't.

He hadn't been this far from home since before he'd become Chace Haig, and even in that time he'd largely been assigned to Europe.

So Chace merely appreciated her. And noted that her accent was pure Los Angeles. And she had that tanned brightness that he'd missed with the others. Granted, most of the folks he'd dealt with at these things were men. Middle-aged, frequently dumpy and rumpled, because the important managers had earned their bones and stayed home.

"What brings you?" he asked.

While the hotel was just that, it also catered to the business crowd, rather than the pure tourists in town for the sights.

"Needed some downtime from the grind," she said, sounding like an American, even dressed as a modern Chinese woman in a snappy jacket and slacks. "Decided to blow off everything and hit Tokyo."

"Understand that feeling," Chace agreed. "My boss told me to take a few weeks and disappear after the last contract got wrapped up so successfully. And to stay out of Switzerland."

"You are Swiss?" she asked, seemingly surprised.

"American," he corrected her. "Work for a small Swiss bank with branch offices in most major cities, but I haven't told the locals I'm here. Don't want to have to answer any questions."

"Yes," she said, smiling and nodding knowingly. They tapped glasses in a small toast. "To staying away from work."

They chatted for a while. At one point, he migrated over to grab some bites from the buffet and she moved on to chat with some of the other folks. When he looked up again from her food, she'd been drawn close again by the tides.

"So what does Chace Haig do when he's not hanging out with stuffy salespeople and industrial spies?" she asked.

He shrugged. It was an open assumption that the line between investor and spy was often a thin one, folks with money looking for any advantage they could get, or tidbit they could sell on.

His secrets were kept closer to the vest.

"If you've got a need, I might know a guy," he replied glibly.

It was, after all, something of a catch-phrase in his life, though most of the time they were underworld crooks and needed introductions as they moved up the socioeconomic ladder.

"That sounds interesting," Rowena said, taking a half-step closer and sliding a bit to the side.

He'd found a corner and now they were more or less excluding everyone else. Chace caught a few jealous looks and knowing smiles, but he wasn't here for an affair on vacation. He supposed that many of these men probably were, away from home and on expense accounts that involved entertainment.

He usually lived too monastic a lifestyle, where nobody was allowed to know too much or get too close.

"What kinds of things do you find?" she asked, sounding innocent but there was a layer of something under there that he couldn't identify.

Chace filed it and made a note to send a contact report home later, inquiring.

In this business, honeypots were common. Pretty spies dangled out there for folks to meet, possibly to set them up for blackmail later. Given what he did, there wasn't much someone could blackmail him with, but anyone trying was up to something and Thane could at least identify her employers for him.

"Generally, folks have needs, but don't know where to find something, so they ask people they trust," he offered. "Many of those folks give them my contact information. I take a finder's fee, introduce them, and walk away to let them complete their business."

There. That flair in her eyes. Smart woman, processing things at a high rate and leaping to all sorts of conclusions, many of which were probably accurate, if you squinted just right and turned your head a little sideways.

Chace Haig was a fence for criminals. Easy as that. But we don't say such things in polite company.

"Dangerous things?" she asked in a leading tone that was still SoCal. He shrugged.

"I know people," he deflected. "Or I can find them. Or folks refer business to me. One hell of a rolodex. Things that might be illegal in one jurisdiction might not be under Swiss law."

Ethically, questionable. Legally, pretty much dark gray to black, most of the time.

And exactly why the US and UK governments had set out to create a deep-cover spy sixty years ago. Someone was going to do this. Might as well insert their own middleman so they could track such things.

And maybe show up and arrest everyone at critical moments.

Or launch airstrikes with precision ordinance.

Making the world a safer place. Or something.

He studied her, because Rowena was inviting study, the way she was standing. Proud. Hardbody. Gorgeous face. Deadly eyes.

"Did you have needs that a guy like me might be able to help with?" he asked quietly.

Might as well be up front if it was going to go that direction. Maybe she was just being flirty. Maybe she was serious. Maybe she was working for someone as a honeypot, because Chace understood that a lot of the men around them would brag a lot to impress a beautiful woman. Take her back to their room, and then fall asleep at some point and let her rifle through whatever paperwork or electronics they had.

Industrial espionage was just spies reporting to companies instead of governments. He'd met one woman who had been a tall, busty redhead who could put on the act of a bubbly airhead at an engineering conference. You'd never know she had a PhD in aeronautical engineering. She'd had a fantastic career for many years on the West Coast of the US, between the plants and engineers in Seattle and Los Angeles.

Los Angeles? Hmmmm.

"I'm not sure," Rowena replied just as quietly. "Just got into town and didn't have any pressing business to attend to, so my needs might be personal rather than professional."

He nodded and kept a polite distance. Might be more flirting. Might be a quiet warning. Or an opening to an invitation. Nothing that mattered to him.

She paused as if in thought. He sipped some of his sidecar, noting that he was about done and would either need to get a second, which he rarely did, or call it an evening and go back to his room to fill out a report on Ms. Rowena Cai and ask Thane to run her through a few systems, just in case.

She turned to look at him from suddenly close enough to dance. Her eyes lit up as if with some sudden thought, but this didn't look like a woman who did anything impulsively.

"What about you?" she countered neatly. "What do you do when you're on vacation?"

"Did a little shopping yesterday," he said. "Found a few things for myself and saw a few sights around town. Mostly, I've stayed in my room or down by the pool while I decompressed. Tomorrow night, I was leaning towards asking the concierge for recommendations and reservations for a steak house down in Ginza, just to get out and see more of the town."

Chace left it hanging there, mostly to see if she'd take the bait.

Was it bait? Maybe. Or maybe it was just general flirtatiousness. He had hardly done anything in two years that wasn't mission oriented, one way or another. Even attending Christmas parties in London was on the job, when he'd helped some mid-ranking Russian mobsters learn how to be more English. And made a whole new set of connections with others that would want introductions.

"Do you know any such places?" she asked.

"Nope," Chace admitted. "That's why I was going to ask them. Anyplace I'd draw would be random. I'd rather find one of those hole-in-the-wall joints that should have gotten a Micheline star at some point, but nobody knew about it. Know any places like that?"

Again, pushing, but only so far as she was leaving openings. It was almost a Tango. Or, given the way she moved, more like Touch-Hands drills.

The original Chace Haig had studied Okinawan martial arts, back in the days when American soldiers and marines were just starting to do so while being stationed there. Mostly karate. Later, he'd supplemented that with Taiwanese forms, largely Hsing-I and Bagua, with a little Tai Chi Chuan thrown in.

The northerners fleeing in 1949 had lost everything, left behind on the mainland, but had brought their knowledge with them, as well as a strong martial mindset and a deep desire to strike back at the Chinese Communist Party, the CCP that Americans had labeled a Yellow Menace, back when such overt racism was acceptable. It was less public today, but still there in a lot of places.

The Taiwanese, though, knew a lot about close combat, even as the CCP and Mainlanders had been purged for knowing such things. Touch-Hands involved literally placing the backs of wrists together and developing the softness to detect any sudden movement or attack from your opponent as soon as they thought of it. You shifted your body and weight loosely around, avoiding the blow and possibly counter-attacking.

Masters of the forms might simply be waving hands back and forth, until you saw the amount of sweat on their brows. And watched someone finally make a mistake that ended up with a body flying across the room. Meanest, most dangerous man Chace had ever met had been barely five feet tall, possibly one hundred pounds, and eighty years old. Skin like leather left out in the sun for years.

And the softest touch of any Human Chace had ever encountered. That, and he routinely threw burly young marines across the room to faceplant on a mat somewhere, head shaking as they tried to figure out what had happened.

"I might know a place," she said with a sly grin.

"That's usually my line," he grinned back.

"I'm stealing it," Rowena countered. "Or borrowing it. You feel like placing yourself in my hands tomorrow night?"

"Am I safe, alone with you?" he countered, ratcheting up the teasing a notch to see where she was going.

"Probably not," she nodded solemnly, eyes still twinkling with an internal laughter. "But if you think I'm too dangerous..."

"You might be," Chace said, studying her again. "But I enjoy a challenge. Keeps me in shape. When should I be ready, where should I be, and how should I be dressed?"

She leaned back to study him like a side of meat. Chace knew he was tall and skinny, especially compared to modern folks, because the original man had been, and Americans had gotten so much heavier over the last two generations.

Still, he did daily exercises, worked the hotel machines, and did kata and forms in his rooms at night, alone so nobody could see what he was up to.

"That sort of outfit," she told him. "Eight PM. Down in the lobby. I have friends in town that will arrange reservations for us and send a car."

Chace nodded.

"Sounds like a deal," he said, careful to not use the word date.

Wasn't a date. Was dinner with a potential contact. Who happened to be a beautiful young woman who might have more money and contacts than he'd have guessed an hour ago. Especially if she could arrange something like that on the fly between now and then.

They shared a smile and he watched her move off, finishing his own drink and then departing.

He needed to file a report with Thane. Standard operating proce-dure, but this one felt like the opening to something bigger.

Hopefully, it wasn't about to ruin his vacation.

CHAPTER
SIX

Zheng Ru-Chen—generally known as "Dragon Scholar Zheng"—studied the street from the safety of a dark alley. It was the Ginza, so not that dark, but he was largely out of sight as the crowds ebbed and flowed around him.

He checked his watch, an old-fashioned mechanical with a battery, because electronics could not always be trusted. Especially not the modern ones, that wanted to connect to any and every open network they found, in order to call their corporate masters and report on someone.

That was a good way to get yourself killed in this business. Especially in Tokyo.

Contacts had whispered a secret, like little birds on a wire gossiping. A time, a place, and a name. Two names, but one was a stranger when he'd been handed the observer files by Manager Kwok.

The traffic of pedestrians was thick tonight, in spite of a slight drizzle that had swept in this afternoon. Ru-Chen let them cover him as he saw a private black car arrive at the restaurant, with the doormen springing into action to get the passengers out.

Cai Chin-Bin emerged first. Ru-Chen didn't have a camera with him. There was a second team taking pictures and video from the safety of a nearby third story office. Ru-Chen was merely observing, because her arrival had triggered quiet alarms, though nothing official with the Japanese government.

Merely those Taiwanese agencies tasked with tracking Mainlander spies and terrorists and not necessarily telling the politicians in the Diet anything unnecessarily.

A man emerged after Cai. Westerner. Hard to tell if he was American or French, as he moved with an odd mix of style and fashion. Tall. Dark. Handsome by western standards. Lean. Moved with deadly care as Cai hooked elbows with the stranger and drew him into the restaurant.

From the body language, this thing wasn't sure if it was a date or a business meeting, as the woman was inciting all of the physical contact, but the man wasn't aggressive or passive. Merely careful as the two walked. There might be a nightcap and sex later, but Ru-Chen wasn't sure if the man was a contact, a victim, or a customer yet.

The two got into the steak house as the car left. The doormen returned to their spots guarding the place. Not a Yakuza gathering place, but one owned at a few legal removes, and thus barely open to the general public.

If you could somehow arrange a reservation. Especially at the last minute.

Ru-Chen knew that Cai had only been in country for forty-eight hours at this point, so this was a sudden, special event. One that warranted closer observation than normal. Pity that he couldn't get inside to somehow eavesdrop on things, but that would cause too many questions.

Instead, he faded back to his alley and pulled out his phone, dialing.

"Status?" Manager Kwok asked immediately.

"They have arrived," Ru-Chen replied. "Cai and the western male. Meeting seems more business than social, but a mix of both. Possibly recruiting. Or entertaining a client."

"I have video coming in, along with photographs," Kwok said. "Maintain your surveillance and we will see if we have the male in our records."

"Should I prepare for active measures?" Ru-Chen asked.

"Stand by, Dragon Scholar," Kwok chuckled. "She might have

flown to town to meet secretly with a new boyfriend, in which case we'll want to take his life apart before doing anything rash."

Ru-Chen suppressed his sigh to silence, knowing that he had something of a reputation around the division for aggressiveness. Necessary, as the Civil War had never really ended, as such things might be measured. They had lost the mainland, and then gone on to fight for the various islands and seas for the last seventy-five years, drawing in the Americans, the Koreans, and the Japanese to help as they went. More recently, the Vietnamese and Filipinos had both decided that Xi and the PRC represented something of an existential threat politically, even as everyone continued to do as much business as one might safely handle.

"I will be prepared," Ru-Chen replied to his boss, without going into any specific details about what he might have prepared.

Manager Kwok cut the line and Ru-Chen dialed a different number. "Sir?"

"Advance your alert status one step," Ru-Chen ordered the rest of his team. "Stand by to assault or capture the criminal Cai, but we await orders from headquarters. They will wait, as is normal, until the last possible moment to act, so we must be poised for violence if the order comes."

"Understood, sir."

Ru-Chen pocketed it phone and went back to watching.

What had drawn the tiger lady from her forests and brought her to Tokyo?

CHAPTER
SEVEN

Chace had adopted a relaxed tone largely at odds with most Asian cultures tonight. Helped that Rowena had spent her high school and college years in Los Angeles. She straddled several cultures in much the same way he did, though almost completely different places.

Chace had some spent time in Southern California, mostly arranging deals for folks that had sought to launder their money by investing in movies. A few had even gotten richer, but mostly they had found ways around most of the tax laws the US liked to impose on the rest of humanity, given any opportunity.

Primarily, he operated out of the US Northeast and northwest Europe.

So he was having fun as Rowena explained things to him. American cities large enough had the sort of performance art that saw folks seated around a table while a chef put on a performance in front of them, chopping, cooking, and filling bowls randomly as they went. This joint had such things going on, but she had gotten them a semi-private booth well off to one side from the tourists, with tall backs that contained all conversations remarkably well. More of a traditional restaurant, and less performance.

Chace was reminded of old mafia roadhouses that still existed architecturally in many places. No windows. Tall booths. Sixties leather and dark interiors.

Not quite Central Casting here, but close.

He sat across from her and sipped sake that was good enough to impress Chace's rather pedestrian taste buds. He'd noted a full bar when he came in, so a sidecar would be next, unless tea intruded.

Small talk had been vague and non-threatening. Rowena wore a pants suit outfit that showed off almost no flesh, while simultaneously emphasizing all the right places to see curves and muscles that many Asian cultures didn't necessarily approve of.

Women were still something of second-class citizens in many countries, and the men simply didn't understand how angry that made their wives and daughters.

Chace figured that the reckoning, already under way, would see most of these countries halve their populations over his lifetime, as parents often didn't get grandchildren. Rowena Cai certainly didn't look like the sort of woman to settle for some businessman. Even a tycoon.

Any man she ended up marrying would be a sidekick, and would have to understand his role well, and be settled to it. Weren't that many men good enough to be a partner to her, and Chace didn't get the impression that he was auditioning.

Not for that, anyway. Lots of questions, mostly skirting around the illegal things he did in his cover identity, without probing too deeply. He wondered if she was the kind of woman who got turned on by that sort of thing. He'd known a few in his time. That, or the prototypical bored housewife—or whatever she did—looking to break out of a rut, like many of those men back at the hotel.

His was a life of danger and excitement, but generally only when things went wrong.

"And what do you do these days?" he asked, as she finished a story about her time at USC and the hijinks that college kids with too much money and too little adult supervision got into.

The man who would become Chace Haig had gone to Yale for his undergrad, and worked his ass off, planning to go to Law School and eventually get into government somewhere.

He had, just not the way he'd expected. Or the man.

"These days?" she asked, slightly taken aback possibly because he hadn't dug in too deep before now. "My father owns a holding company in Hong Kong. Mostly he invests in lots of smaller companies. All of my siblings but one work for him in some capacity."

Chace nodded. The casual way she said it suggested old Cantonese money, quietly hiding from the Party. And lots of it, if she had gone to USC. Possibly descended from smugglers, if smuggling had ever really stopped. He remembered reading a study written in the late '80s that mentioned trade as a percent of GDP in Hong Kong had actually been above one hundred percent, mostly because officially declared numbers in various market sectors never came close to matching up, and the British hadn't pressed too had to answer questions about that golden goose. Then it had stopped being their problem, and Beijing got to deal with it instead.

And her father had had the money and connections to send at least one daughter to the University of Southern California for a degree in business, with a minor in English Lit. That had been where *Rowena* came from, a character in Scott's *Ivanhoe*.

Chace assumed shipping. And smuggling. Thane would need a few days to dig up anything useful, assuming the usual tidbits, but he'd dutifully filed reports before coming, so she knew where to start looking if he disappeared.

Paranoia was a lifestyle in this business. Rowena gave off a lot of the same vibes, as he started really honing in on her speech patterns.

"So what do you want to be when you grow up?" he pressed. "What would you do if you had all the money in the world and no responsibilities for it?"

It was a great question to ask at parties, because it forced people to step out of their mundane lives and expose the artist underneath, if only for a few seconds. And it let him understand them, when he might want to bribe them later.

Rowena went cold and studied him. It was almost like a different person sat across from him for a second, before the two women he'd seen changed places back again. Fast as a blink, but he'd seen in. Chace kept his face perfectly neutral and smiled expectantly at her.

"I'd dance," she said quietly. "My brother chucked it all and became a painter. Sometimes, I think he's the only one of us really happy. The rest settled for rich. You?"

Chace nodded. He had a pretty good idea what *rich* meant in her context now.

"I'd buy a big truck that could double as a camper," he offered. "Wander around North and maybe South America, stopping at various places to see the sights and meet people, then heading on to the next place."

"You should have been a cowboy?" she grinned. "Nineteenth century wanderer?"

"Something like that," he agreed. "The job keeps me moving around, but I'm always hustling, like a shark that will drown if it ever stops swimming. I'd forgotten how to take time off and relax. That was why the boss sent me on vacation for a few weeks. It's been years."

"Same," she replied in a wistful tone. "After USC, I went home and have worked for the family business for almost five years now."

Food interrupted at that moment, so they dropped the serious talk and shifted back to safer ground. But there was something in her eyes that he couldn't identify.

Not yet, anyway.

Ru-Chen answered on the second ring, but he'd been poised. And a little damp, but hats weren't a common fashion statement this year, so he'd had to stay back as close to the building as he could to try to stay dry as the rain came and went.

Manager Kwok.

"Sir?"

"The man is confirmed as Chace Haig," Kwok began without preamble. "He is a fence that normally works Europe and the Middle East, dealing with a variety of criminal underworld elements and terrorist organizations. Did you see evidence that he was armed?"

"Negative," Ru-Chen replied. "However, we only saw him from the car to the door, and you've had better optics than we did. It is Japan, though."

"Agreed," Kwok noted. "As he arrived publicly, we might assume that he could not have a gun. However, he has also been here for several days, and met with various people, both in town at the hotel, so you should be prepared."

"Your orders, sir?" Ru-Chen asked, his heart rate suddenly stepping up as adrenaline got dumped into his system.

"Make it look like a Yakuza hit, Dragon Scholar," Kwok ordered. "Cai cannot be up to anything good if she has brought such a man to Tokyo secretly. They must have thought that they could slip past our guard by using Japanese businessmen as a cover. Whatever she is buying or selling to the man needs to be disrupted, especially as Chairman Xi is rattling his saber again and threatening to invade our home."

"Have they made concrete movements?" Ru-Chen asked, shocked.

"Not yet, but Cai meeting with Haig opens a whole new side of things and we don't have time to explore it in more depth. The KMT has a long memory, regardless of who is in power in Tainan. The communists will not rest until they finally win the civil war, either by invading Taiwan, or using nuclear weapons to destroy it. Since we cannot be certain what Haig is being hired for, he must be eliminated."

"And Cai, Manager?" Ru-Chen asked, unwilling to get his hopes too high.

"Collateral damage, Dragon Scholar."

Ru-Chen smiled and touched the pistol under his arm for luck.

If she hadn't been concerned about some of the falseness about the man, Rowena could have seen recruiting Chace. For any number of things, not all of which were necessarily about business. As it was, she'd adroitly dropped hints about perhaps taking her back up to his room and fooling around after dinner.

Better, he'd just as delicately danced around such things without ever committing. Or turning her down.

How long had it been since she'd had someone she could flirt so much with, then actually consider consummating things afterwards?

And she still didn't know if he was somehow connected with the man who had shot her father. Certainly, it hadn't been Chace, as he'd only been born two years later. Hardly a spy and assassin while still in diapers, though Chun-Bin had started studying martial arts at age five, even as many students were years older when they began.

Chace had been a most interesting conversationalist at dinner. And handsome. Smart. Fun.

She found herself looking forward to fencing more with the man, once they got back to the hotel.

Rowena had his arm in hers as they exited the restaurant, laughing at another one of his sly observations about folks they had passed on the way out. Chace had the ability to glance at someone, analyze them, then make up a story about them at the drop of a hat.

Had he been born Japanese, she had no doubts that he'd be the man forever winning haiku contests, where you had to adapt something someone else had said, on the fly, and make it both funny and deeply philosophical.

The door was opened for them and they emerged into Tokyo's night. It had rained while they'd been indoors, a good washing that left everything damp and cool, before it would no doubt ramp up the humidity terribly tomorrow. Sounded like a good reason to lay about the pool as Chace had done, and not just so she could show off her hard body to a man that was expressing how impressed he was with her.

Unlike most of the men she ever met, who either feared her or saw her as a tool to advance their own careers.

Dull, pointless men.

She felt Chace turn sharply and tense in ways that weren't immediately obvious, save that she had pressed herself against his side in flirty ways while laughing. Teasing. Offering, perhaps, as they had so carefully played up until now, just heightening the anticipation she felt for an evening of more fun.

She started to turn, interested in what had drawn his attention away from the car waiting for them at the curb, but Chace moved.

One moment, poised. The next, she was thrust forward and away and would have fallen as she bounced off people walking by, save for her training.

Simultaneously, he called a single word and surged into another man walking up.

"Down!" he ordered.

Then the gunshot rang out.

Tokyo's night suddenly smelled like danger. There was no other way for Chace to describe it, past that. Unconscious cues locked his head into certain patterns before he even understood what was happening.

The night sounds had changed.

A hand reached for the gun he hadn't brought to Japan. He saw the man walking forward with an intent that made the stranger stand out against the crowd of civilians walking past. They were little fish schooling and shoaling as they went, moving around rocks and sharks.

The stranger moved like a shark.

"Down," he said to Rowena, twisting and using his hips to sling her forward and out of the way of the gunman, because Chace suddenly saw the pistol in the man's hand.

Low at his side as he walked, arm not swinging, which was what had made him stand out in that instant when Chace had scanned the crowd outside. Damp hair, cut short, like a man who had been standing out in the rain, watching. Waiting. Chinese face. Northern bones.

Chace exploded into motion. That was how you dealt with such a situation.

It was impossible to dodge a bullet, so you don't try. Instead, you dodge the shooter. He must bring the weapon up and aim it. The better the gunman, the faster they could do such a thing.

Running just meant that you got shot in the back. Or the back of the head, considering how much taller Chace was than most of this crowd.

The gunman hadn't been expecting Chace to charge him. Or had been watching Rowena and expecting her to do something, because he'd shifted his shoulders and hips when she moved forward.

Right hand shooter. Body twisting with the natural flow right-to-left. He had to break that to react, shifting his weight back against his body in order to bring the gun up.

Chace was on top of him before the man could shoot.

Or rather, aim.

First bullet went into the pavement at their feet. Chace didn't feel any tug of a ricochet, so hopefully it had gone in instead of bouncing into an innocent civilian.

Chace attacked the gun arm.

The man had training in close combat forms, because he automatically brought the pistol up like a sai or knife used defensively.

Chace spoofed at his face, then unloaded with everything he had into the man's elbow. Funny bone strike. Meanest practical joke in the world, when sparring on a mat with people you like.

Or at least respect.

Shooter's arm went numb from the way nerveless fingers suddenly weren't holding the gun anymore.

Chace kept up his charge, aiming for a step just past the man, then planting his left foot and rotating backwards with a motion a parkour expert had refined into him last year. Almost a ballet of violence, because frequently those folks encountered angry security guards protecting properties that the athletes want to challenge.

Right hand catches the gun, already starting to fall as the shoulders rotate, led by the hips. Left hand impacts the back of the man's neck, then catches hold. Left leg provides an anchor point point to drive muscles. Right leg is an axle, an axis of rotation, and a fulcrum across which the shooter's motion is interdicted.

He cannot step, because his leg encounters Chace's foot when it comes forward, then his head is leading the rest of him over the wall of Chace's leg, and the man is falling.

There wasn't a wall close by for Chace to bounce the shooter off of. Or a car, which was the other direction.

Chace settled for throwing him down, then following, pouncing on the man like a hungry cat. The pistol was gripped by the top of the barrel, and felt like a Glock, so Chace used it like a hammer to bash the man in the side of the neck. Soft spot, wherever you hit, likely to render him stunned if not unconscious, but not killing him like a blow to the temple or ear might do.

It was Japan, and they would throw a fit, once they had arrested him, even if certain whispers were sent into certain ears and the government had to sweep it all under the rug.

Motion.

Chace was up, turning, and holding the Glock left handed as two other men emerged from the mass of fishies around him, both also drawing weapons from shoulder holsters and looking like the sorts of folks Chace occasionally had to get into gunfights with.

But this was Tokyo. Ginza, even. What the hell was going on? Why were they trying to kill him? Except that the first shooter had been paying more attention to Rowena, like she was supposed to be the dangerous one, while Chace was just a Swiss Banker, right?

Wrong.

Chace shot the closer gunman in the thigh. He had no idea who these people were, or why they were trying to kill him. Or Rowena.

He'd say in broad daylight, but it was Tokyo's night, and damp, so it kind of ruined the metaphor, even as it hit the exact image of how Westerners always saw Tokyo in the movies.

Second shooter went down. Third shooter ducked back into the crowd.

The people around them finally woke up to gunshots in their midst and lost their shit.

Chace had never run the bulls in Spain. That was a gig for morons and rush junkies. At least nobody here had horns.

It was still a mad stampede of bodies screaming and going every which way. Mindless, because it takes training to know what to do when someone is trying to kill you.

Third shooter got tackled by a woman less than half his size and twice his age, but Chace didn't think she was a hero. Merely running, and would have slammed into a telephone pole just as easily. Telephone pole wouldn't have gone down, though.

Third shooter was on the sidewalk. Chace turned and located Rowena.

For about a half an eyeblink, he considered the black car, but the streets had been so full of cars and pedestrians that they might walk back to the hotel faster. He ignored it, however much that open rear door called to him of safety, and grabbed Rowena by the hand.

She resisted for a moment, then moved as he pulled her along.

"Your enemies or mine?" she asked as they started to run away from the screaming and sound of sirens and whistles.

Chace pulled her ahead of him, since she knew these streets and he didn't.

"I have no idea," he said, pushing her to move. "Nor do I wish to find out, or get arrested. The folks at the restaurant won't say anything to the cops, will they?"

"Not if they know what's good for them," she acknowledged, starting to use her own shoulders and elbows to open a space to move.

Chace relied on his mass, and a willingness to hip-check folks moving slower, because they were running without any destination in mind safe perceived safety, whether that was into a building or down into the subway tunnels.

Chace started to let go of Rowena's hand, but she clamped on tighter so he kept up. That woman could move.

It was a little weird, holding her right hand and a Glock left-handed. He kept it down at his side like the shooter had. They moved like dancers in an avalanche of bodies, down a subway staircase, and into the bowels of the earth.

CHAPTER
ELEVEN

Rowena had seen Chace move. Suddenly explode into action against the assassin, then ruthlessly take out two others as if it was a matter of course.

Who was this man?

At least she believed him to be a killer now. Not merely a banker. One banker does not take out three killers by himself in the blink of an eye. Even she would have been hard pressed in that situation.

Then he grabbed her hand and dragged her deeper into the crowd.

They ran.

She kept hold of him when he might have slipped away from her, because Rowena had questions Chace Haig needed to answer.

Whether she would like his answers was an entirely different question.

Into the subway, ahead of the rest of the mad rush of people like a surfer riding the perfect eighth of eights wave that came along every once in a while.

Rowena missed surfing, but it wasn't a Chinese thing. Still, the metaphor shaped her as she dodged bodies descending. Find the perfect balance point to slide in and out. She'd never really driven cars that much, but had gearhead friends, and the vocabulary was similar.

They hit the platform at the bottom without breaking stride and she tugged him into a car that was just filling with people. Somewhere, the gun had disappeared, but she found it again when she got pressed tight up against him in the mob. Jacket pocket. Still in his hand, in case he needed to draw and fire again.

In Tokyo? Who the hell hated her this much in Japan? Or were they after Chace?

He hadn't been sure. Had asked if they were his enemies or hers.

Rowena had no clue at the moment, merely the need to move. To get away from whatever was happening before she could be boxed in by someone dangerous enough to matter.

Though she supposed that she had a tiger in the room with her. Hopefully, it would be hungry for someone else.

Chace leaned down like he was smelling her hair, which put his mouth to her ear. Rowena leaned in and pressed herself against him like this was a date. Anything to not register with the folks in the subway car who might be interviewed later.

There were always cameras recording things. They didn't prevent crime, but could solve almost anything if someone was patient enough to string video together from enough sources.

"Is the hotel safe?" he asked.

Rowena considered her options.

"Probably not," she said simply. "That was a professional hit, but they should have used a sniper."

"Agreed," he said. "Someone wanted to make it look like a gangland hit. At least in Europe or the US. Does Japan do it that way?"

"Sometimes," she agreed. "Far less common."

"I don't know Tokyo except as a one-week old tourist," he offered. "Where might be safe?"

"If they knew where to find one of us, I would presume they could track us electronically," she said.

"Put your phone on airplane mode," he said. "Or turn it off entirely. Where can we find a burner at this time of night?"

She considered. And listened to his words and tones.

This was not the same man she'd been flirting with an hour ago. Not that banker with perhaps a checkered past.

Chace Haig was a killer, but you didn't ever get to see that. Unless you started something, she supposed.

He did look and sound more like the sort of man who could have shot her father, thirty-five year ago, though.

Spy? Something.

And she couldn't ask him the truth. Not right now. Not while someone was hunting them. One of them, anyway. But that just meant both, until they were safe. Or separated.

And Chace had carefully not killed any of those three men. He could use violence as a precise tool and an art form. She filed that away, seeing herself in that same mirror, when so few others ever did.

Still, he was right. She got the phone and shut it down, then thought about Tokyo.

They'd grabbed the first car leaving, destination unknown, and Tokyo wasn't where she normally operated, but he'd asked her for help.

And it would help both of them.

"Two stops," she replied. "There should be shops open that we can visit. I didn't bring a purse because I wouldn't need it there."

"I've got cash," he said simply, nodding.

And he said it in such a way that suggested he was used to suddenly needing to pay for something without using a card of any kind. No records.

Where had she heard that before?

"Who can you call?" Rowena asked, aware that he didn't know many people in Japan. Supposedly.

That was why he'd chosen it, at least according to the cover story he'd given her.

Cover story? Had she already decided that the man was a spy for someone?

Yes. Who?

That was the interesting question.

"I have contacts," Chace murmured a little evasively. "I'll reach out to one of them and invoke some favors. They owe me and would love nothing more than to repay to debts previously incurred."

Debts. Honor. Again, something she understood perhaps deeper than most. Who would he call?

Rowena nodded and let it go at that. Eventually, she would need to dig deeper into his life and find out more of his secrets, but right now they were being hunted by someone and she needed his help to escape.

Then, she would start hunting them back.

CHAPTER
TWELVE

Chace rode to the second stop pressed up against Rowena. It was a pleasant feeling, though all thoughts of fooling around later had evaporated.

He'd gone tactical. And she was looking at him with new eyes, but that couldn't be helped. If anything, he would need to dig deeper into who she really was and determine why she had picked him out of a crowd to seduce.

And it wasn't her ambush. That gunman had been more focused on her than him, in that split second when he'd made the wrong choice about who to engage first. Someone hunting her, and he'd happened to be along for the ride.

Right now, ditching her and vanishing sounded like a wise move, but he didn't have the contacts he needed in Japan.

And Chace wanted to know more about Rowena Cai. If he vanished, he'd likely never get those answers. There were deep currents running here, and Chace wanted answers.

Second stop, she was in motion, drawing him in her wake. He had the Glock tucked into a pocket, but hadn't had the opportunity to study it in any detail. A quick glance had suggested a Gen 5 Glock 19, but there were so many possible variants of the weapon that he didn't know how many rounds he might have short of pulling the magazine to count them, which you didn't do on a Japanese train.

Two shots down from wherever he had started, so he had at least eight more, and probably fifteen, if he was dumb enough to get into a firefight with someone on the streets and back alleys of Tokyo.

In his wallet, he had one million yen tucked away. Ballpark around seven thousand US dollars, depending on the exchange rate tonight.

Enough.

He needed a phone. One call, and he could get a lot of things into motion that would take care of most of his needs.

What did he need?

Answers.

Someone had tried to kill the two of them. And one of her enemies, Chace was certain of that, because the man had been surprised to have Chace attacking.

Someone who didn't know who he was. Or thought he was just another Swiss banker.

Chace nodded to himself as the doors opened and they flowed into the crowd, out and up and out onto the streets.

He knew roughly where he was from studying the subway map, but that was cartographical knowledge, and not geographical. He had no idea what kind of neighborhood it would be, but there were a lot of bright lights and folks moving around on the sidewalks.

Rowena pulled him up to a kiosk shop that might have been six square meters, with a man behind a counter and boxes behind him. Cell phone boxes. Lots of them.

The man had a wary eye for Chace, but seemed to know Rowena as they approached. Chace wasn't conversational in Japanese, but he picked out words as she addressed the man.

More studying. Chace stood still and let the man see the shell he wore as a disguise.

"What kind phone?" the shopkeeper asked in broken English.

"Mid-range," Chace replied. "Android. Prepaid. Able to call anywhere in Japan. Immediately active so I can call someone."

He left it at that. The shopkeeper turned to Rowena and a faster conversation ensued. Dickering about price.

Chace looked at hand-drawn price stickers on the wall behind the man. To make a point, he pulled out his wallet, putting seventy-five thousand yen on the counter between them and letting the man see that he had more. Around five hundred US.

He assumed that he'd be getting something crappy, but all he needed was to make one phone call. Possibly receive one as well, but maybe not. Then he'd drop it in a trash can when he was done.

Money was an international language.

The shopkeeper grunted, turning and pulling a box from the wall behind him. Opening it, the man slipped a SIM card in and powered it up, waiting as it cheerfully did that silly boot-up song and dance that phone companies programmed.

Sixty thousand yen disappeared and the man shoved the rest back. Chace nodded and glanced at Rowena before slipping the rest into his pocket. The cost and the bribe had been less than he'd expected, but having ready cash and Rowena was probably the difference tonight.

Rowena had made a lot of differences tonight, but he wanted answers before he burned her and disappeared.

"Is good?" the man asked.

"Is perfect," Rowena said, drawing Chace away from the kiosk and back into the crowd.

He let her lead him to an alley nearby as the phone finally locked in and became part of the cellular universe.

"What do you need next?" she asked.

"Watch the crowd for trouble while I make a call," Chace replied.

In a pinch, he'd drop the phone, draw the Glock, and deal with the consequences later.

Or not.

He dialed as she turned away from him.

The woman was smart. She would learn too much about Chace Haig doing this, but he needed her for now. Maybe needed to have her brought in and arrested. Or at least disappeared into the depths of the hungry international intelligence apparatus he was about to activate.

He dialed the number from memory. Always from memory. No phone ever had anybody's name or number programmed in, and he routinely deleted call records in case somebody got hold of any device he'd used.

It rang twice.

"Hallenbeck Services, how may I route your call?" a young woman with a mid-Atlantic accent answered in English. Even in Japan.

"This is Chace Haig," he replied. "H-A-I-G. Calling on an unsecured device. The password is Quartz."

He waited as she typed, knowing that he had just set off a bomb in certain quarters, because this was his emergency number, to be used only in the most drastic of situations.

Like being hunted by assassins in the back alleys of Tokyo.

"Good evening, Mr. Haig," she replied. "Quartz noted. What do you need?"

Quick.

"I need a safe house where two of us can disappear from trouble," Chace replied, watching that information ripple through Rowena's shoulders as she listened in on his half of the conversation. "Directions or I need someone to pick us up."

He gave the woman a rough location, being two blocks north of the subway station, but he would be in motion as soon as he ended the call, and they knew that.

Procedures, with someone likely flipping open a manual as she spoke and following a much more interesting call system logic tree than you ever got with a normal help line.

"Transport is in motion, being vectored down north of you," she replied. "Urban or removed?"

Chace considered his options. Urban meant staying close to the center of Tokyo. Useful, if he needed to get out of the country quickly. Risky, because he'd still stand out among Japanese folks.

"Removed from the city," he decided.

That also let him isolate Rowena Cai and see if he could get more information out of her, before he had to burn her entirely. Hell of a woman. Be a dreadful shame to burn that bridge without a damned good reason.

Better than he had right now.

"Noted, Mr. Haig," the operator said. "Hanging up now. Next call will be your ride."

"Thank you," he said, then he was talking to himself.

The phone went into his other pocket, opposite the Glock.

Rowena shifted back to stand beside him, still watching the crowd walking by.

"You have interesting friends," she observed neutrally.

"Dangerous ones," he corrected her. "But they owe me favors. This is one of those times where I had to call them in. Do you want to walk away right now? You know this town far better than I do."

"And I have no idea who sent killers after us."

"They were after you," Chace said, gambling a little that those sorts of tidbits now might loosen her up later, when he needed the truth.

Or at least close enough to the truth.

"You are certain?" she asked, but her voice didn't deny it.

"He tracked you instead of me in that instant," Chace nodded, eyes still forward though he could watch her out of the corner of his eye. "That was his mistake."

"Because you are a much more dangerous man than you let on," she completed the thought.

Chace didn't deny it. She'd seen too much. Might know too much.

At the same time, she'd seemed surprised at how dangerous he was, so this woman didn't really know who he was.

That worked in his favor as well.

"Who are you?" she asked, turning more of her body to face him, even as her eyes stayed on the people.

"A guy with dangerous friends," he offered, staying in that top level cover of a guy who found things for dangerous people.

And occasionally got into firefights with yahoos, but she didn't need to know more than she already did.

"You've done this before," she continued, not asking a question by making it a statement.

"A time or two," he allowed.

If you kept things to the last month or three. Going farther back, those numbers went up rather rapidly.

Chace Haig wasn't supposed to be an assassin. The Institute had people specifically trained for that sort of thing, whether it was car bombs, impossible rifle shots, or poisons in food.

His job was to find people. Find things for people, but the sorts of people who needed those sorts of things were folks that Thane and her bosses wanted to know. To track.

Occasionally, to eliminate, either with prison or death.

Sometimes, he still had to get into firefights with yahoos.

"I think I'm safer with you," Rowena told him. "At least until I can contact my people and find a way to slip out of town."

"We'll be out of town," he said. "Do you need to be extracted from the country?"

"I might," she replied, grinning slyly. "Know anybody I might call about arranging that sort of thing?"

"I might know a guy," he grinned back, feeling the emotional signature in the alley shift away from what it had been a moment ago.

Not back to playful and flirty, but not as heavy—not as dark—as it had been.

"Then I should make sure I keep you around for a while, Chace," she nodded. "Never know how useful you might be."

He let that one go. This woman had secrets that he needed to plumb while he had her handy.

And he might even enjoy the experience.

At least for a while.

CHAPTER
THIRTEEN

Rowena contemplated her own phone. She'd dropped a new card in it when traveling to Japan, but had all her contacts. As Chace had said, however, she didn't know who had set her up. And he was dead certain they'd been after her.

He nodded as they relaxed some, then let him take her hand and guide her out into traffic, headed north on foot, though she wasn't sure where they were going. Whoever he had spoken to on his burner phone had been prompt, crisp, and starkly professional. Like he'd made all these arrangements ahead of time.

She didn't think he was a mole sent to infiltrate her father's organization. Chace had shot one of them and brutally beaten a second, which didn't sound believable just to insert a spy.

Ergo, he was a spy, but not one aimed at her.

Possibly.

Had her father overreacted and drawn Chace into his orbit without realizing it? After all, the name Chace Haig was one that had conjured anger from the Chairman. And this Chace Haig had revealed himself to be no stranger to violence.

They walked, maintaining a watch but not talking as they brushed by various people. The rain had made walking a squelchy sound over a quiet nattering hum. Rain jackets rustled with that plasticy sound they did when you moved. Music played, but quietly, as if unwilling to argue with the rain for precedent.

Far fewer smells, once you got past *wet*. Everything knocked down and not recovered. Rowena didn't want to admit to feeling something similar, but the assassination attempt had jarred her off-center, in ways that Chace hadn't felt.

He looked and felt like a machine more than a man. Utterly focused. Perfectly lethal, because she had no doubts that he could have killed all three men had that been necessary.

Who was Chace Haig? What was he?

North. Walking. Thinking.

Father had been shot by a man named Chace Haig thirty-five years ago, an event that had saved Deng from being overruled or possibly even deposed, before that man could open all of China to the West.

But Mao's autarky had failed. She had studied enough business in LA to understand that China could have been left to molder and eventually decay into irrelevance had Deng not acted.

That wasn't the same as appreciating the man. He had done the thing he thought would bring China back to the preeminent position they'd once held, when the Middle Kingdom had ruled, even if that was as much fantasy as fact, given the Song, the Yuan, or the Qing.

Father and Grandfather had helped the Party maintain itself in the face of those challenges, as money flooded in and corrupted even the most stalwart cadre in the process of minting billionaires.

And now Chace Haig had come. Or perhaps he'd been minding his own business and she'd involved him in things he had no business knowing.

She wanted to flee. To disappear from his life and sever all connection as a way of protecting her father. At the same time, he had sent her to understand if Chace Haig was a threat.

Had he invoked his own doom instead?

And did she presume that Chace Haig was a direct threat?

Too much to learn, she dared not let the man escape until she understood his secrets.

And maybe killed him for them, if that became necessary later.

His new phone rang. He stopped short, then pulled her sideways, except that he was moving towards the street rather than the safety of a building where they could move out of the foot traffic.

"Haig," he answered, head on a swivel as she did the same.

Rowena didn't see anything standing out. Nobody approaching.

"Understood," Chace continued. "Turn your head to the right. Yes. There. Thirty seconds."

Then he hung up.

She'd been watching him. In the distance, a blacked out sedan had turned its lights on and a man was standing in the open passenger door. Rowena watched the stranger put away a phone and ignore them to watch the pedestrians, just as she had been doing.

All that, from one call? Who was Chace Haig and what sort of resources did he have instantly available?

American spy was the obvious response, given some of his cues. She needed to know more.

More about him. More about who he worked for. More about the threat he represented.

Chace tugged her hand and they began to approach that car.

It felt like there should be ominous music playing, somewhere besides in her head, but she followed the man.

She was about to be committed.

How deep was too deep?

Chace approached the car with care. And a hand out of sight on the Glock, in case he needed to open fire through the jacket, then clear a jam and move sideways into a combat situation.

Japanese male. Low profile. Dark suit. Earpiece in, presumably with a microphone monitoring. One hand also out of sight, but Chace had invoked Quartz, so they would be prepared for a firefight right now.

Presumably, the armor rating on the sedan was rated up to anything considered small arms.

The man turned his head and made eye contact long enough to nod, then went back to watching the crowd. Chace closed.

They stepped close and he turned to study Rowena from close enough that they were practically dancing.

"If you get in the car with me, you will be isolated until we can determine that the situation is safe," he told her. "I have no idea how long that will be, but I know a guy who can make arrangements to get you somewhere safe at some later point. Or you can walk away right now and trust your people to get you home."

He watched the impact his words on her. Not a civilian, because they would have reacted entirely differently. Not formally trained like he had been. Continued to be. Would continue for as long as he was Chace Haig.

Until Thane hired his replacement.

At the same time, the woman was trained and dangerous to a level that was rare in the field. Competent to play in the sorts of leagues he walked.

One hell of a woman, but he couldn't be too certain whose side she was on.

Not until he talked to Thane and found out who Rowena Cai really was.

"I'm not safe on these streets," she said. "Even Tokyo and its crowds, because I have no idea who they are."

He nodded. Perfectly succinct assessment, when most folks would have been emotional. Angry, perhaps. Frightened, likely.

Not calm and professional.

"Door's unlocked," he told her. "You in first."

He rotated in place once, Glock ready to unleash the hounds of hell if necessary, as she opened the door and slid into the back of the sedan.

Chace was in a moment later, pulling the door shut even as the passenger up front did the same and the driver got them into motion, cutting off someone driving.

"Medical needs?" the passenger asked without looking back.

"None at present," Chace replied.

He'd looked at his foot and the ricochet had gone elsewhere.

"In motion, sir," the driver said simply.

Chace leaned back some and felt the car rumble along. Like Weland's Audi, it rode low, but that much armor was heavy. At the same time, it had a lot of power up front, because you needed to outrun folks from time to time. Like that idiot in the Mustang.

Rowena's hand found his and interlaced fingers as she watched him. Shock would be wearing off soon and she'd move on to whatever was the next emotion she needed in order to process things.

Chace would need something to drink. Possibly an herbal tea without caffeine so he could sleep, but he also knew that Quartz would set in motion all sorts of troubles and he'd be answering questions all night.

Especially about the beautiful woman with him.

She asked a variety of silent questions with her face. He shrugged and smiled, unwilling to commit to anything until he felt safer. And he had no idea how far they were going tonight.

There was no music playing. Just fans circulating air and the dull rumble of the tires and the engine. After a time, her breathing slowed and he felt her relax.

Rowena surprised him by leaning onto his shoulder and closing her eyes. Then she fell asleep, or at least meditated heavily enough that it might be the same.

Still, he'd known enough military veterans in his time. They all swore that they'd learned to fall asleep at the flip of a switch, uncertain when they might sleep again.

Up ahead, the lights began to thin as they climbed out into the mountains.

Rowena woke with a start, surprised that she'd fallen asleep. And leaned on Chace. And making a getaway from an assassination attempt.

He smiled wryly. She shared it and sat back upright.

The night had intruded as she'd slept. Far fewer lights than she'd seen before, but Rowena had already determined that she was going to have to trust Chace at some fundamental level if she wanted to learn the truth.

Any of the truth.

Nobody had spoken while she'd been down. Rowena was certain any voices would have brought her back up. Or motion on Chace's point. Ergo, he'd stayed perfectly still.

And she'd subconsciously trusted him that much, so she had to admit that to herself.

The car was climbing into the hills. At one point, it turned down a side road that was darker, then an even-smaller one that felt more like a long driveway than anything. Gravel under the wheels and space for two Kei trucks to pass side by side, but not much more as it almost touched both mirrors.

They pulled into a clearing in front of a house built sturdy, and done in a style she could only classify as English Tudor, which was jarring considering where they were.

She glanced at her...partner? Associate? Contact? How to describe Chace Haig right now?

He shrugged just enough that she felt it in her hands.

So, he didn't know either? Had called someone for help and placed himself into their hands?

Good to know. She'd done the same, and had to trust the man.

Circular drive under a roof. The car came to a stop and Chace opened his door immediately. He slid out without any words spoken. Rowena did the same, watching the vehicle immediately pull away and drive back down the hill and the driveway.

She moved to stand next to Chace, but didn't take his hand, even though that felt right. Natural.

New ground. New battleground? Hard to tell.

The big door opened and a small Japanese woman stood there, dressed in pants and tunic that somehow split the difference between modern Paris and Shogunate Japan. Muted colors.

"Mr. Haig, your rooms are ready," she said quietly, gesturing them closer.

Rowena followed Chase up three steps onto a wide concrete porch. Rooms?

She replayed the conversation in her head and Chace had specified a safe house for two. Did she want her own room?

Rowena had been prepared to seduce the man earlier. Or be seduced by him. A way to get close enough to learn his secrets.

There were already far more secrets being revealed than she had been prepared for.

Inside, the foyer was a compact space, with heavy wooden doors to both sides instead of sliding shoji, continuing the Western theme of the building. Hardwood floor. Landscape watercolors.

The housekeeper led them deeper, through a door to the rear and into a larger room with a staircase up and more doors, all closed. The stairs had a rug that dampened sound, but she already knew that Chace walked silently.

Rowena strove to emulate him as they ascended.

To the right. More paintings and art, all of it with a mixed feeling, as if Japanese and British had been stirred together in a bowl, then poured back out again.

The woman opened a door and gestured.

"The first room," she said. "Self-contained. Clothing is available from stores. How soon did you need to eat?"

"Breakfast," Chace replied as she followed him to the door and looked in.

Front sitting room, done with a couch and a chair. Two doors off, possibly a bathroom and a sleeping room, like a mid-range hotel suite might have done it.

Everything was completely anonymous in that same way that hotels did it.

The housekeeper gestured.

"The other room is directly across the hall," she said. "This wing is currently unoccupied, but we ask that you not wander. Someone will come up for you for breakfast. Japanese, Chinese, or Continental?"

Chace turned to ask her a question from the set his eyes. The woman had recognized her as Chinese that easily? But she'd known the housekeeper to be Japanese.

"Continental," she decided, just to keep things slightly off-kilter.

"Very well," the woman bowed. "Are there any other needs?"

"This." She watched Chace pull out the pistol he'd taken from the gunman earlier, handing it to the housekeeper. "It needs to be cleaned and traced. Probably disappeared somewhere where there won't be any questions. In fact, here's the burner phone. Make it vanish, too, and I'll use your landline to make arrangements.

"Excellent, Mr. Haig," the woman said, taking both and pausing to look at Rowena for a long moment before she departed back up the hallway and disappeared.

"Do you care which side?" Chase asked.

Rowena considered her response.

"Earlier, we were dancing on the verge of sleeping together," she began, to see how he would react, now that she was somehow inside his normal secrecy and learning too much about him.

Too much? Perhaps. Maybe just enough.

What would she need to know to assuage Father?

And what should she do it this Chace Haig turned out to be connected to the one that had shot him?

Chace watched her, trying to determine Rowena's game.

He needed to check in. See what Thane had found. How the Institute would react to a Quartz call from Tokyo.

At the same time, he had been looking forward to getting to know Rowena Cai in a much more robust and interesting manner. Possibly without clothing.

But things had gone dangerous. Tactical.

Professional.

And she was far more than she let on.

At some point, he was going to have to trust her. Or burn her.

Chace had no idea which choice would be more dangerous.

Her eyes held a wealth of emotions as she studied her. Concern for herself. Anger at the ambush. Interest in him. Possibly a need for touch as the mad energy finally collapsed like a soap bubble, alone in the darkness.

"I'm going to have to make a call and explain things to some people," he offered. Not an evasion or a deflection, but a bald statement that didn't explain anything more than she needed. "I have no idea how long that will take, and there are things you don't get to know about that."

He watched that surge of righteous anger rise and fall as she considered his words. She nodded after a moment, understanding that she'd put herself in his hands when he'd given her several opportunities to walk.

Thus, she didn't want to walk.

Why?

Who was Rowena Cai? Who was she working for? Who were her enemies?

Chace wondered if he'd accidentally walked into somebody's game board, somehow turning chess into three-color *Go*.

"What would you like?" he asked simply. "What would make you the most comfortable?"

She considered. Evaluated and discarded a wealth of options faster than anybody who wasn't an agent. But he already knew that much.

And understood that she was at his mercy, such as it was, until he cleared the game board. Or called in more pieces. He saw that in her eyes as well.

She came to a conclusion. He waited.

"I'll take a shower," she said with a shallow nod. "The woman mentioned clothing?"

"Your room will have a phone," he replied. "Pick it up and someone will answer."

"Then maybe I'll try to sleep," Rowena continued. "I sleep light, if you were to slip in later."

Chace understood that for the invitation it was, but didn't know her emotional makeup to know if she'd want to be held, cuddled, or fucked utterly silly. Everybody reacted to stress differently, and most people never got into the sorts of situations where they discovered such things about themselves.

"I'll make my calls," he acknowledged. "Then see where we're at from there. I can't make any promises, because I don't know how long it will take me to explain what I did tonight."

"Understood," she nodded. "You stay here and I'll take the one across the hall."

He considered grabbing her for a quick kiss. Her eyes almost invited it.

Almost.

By silent acknowledgment, she moved away with a shared nod and they both closed their doors.

Chace blew out a heavy breath and moved deeper into the room. The walls and doors would be practically sound-proof, from previous experience with private Agency resorts like this, and someone would monitor the hallway. If she came out to listen, they would alert him.

It was as safe as he could get right now.

Stripping off his jacket, Chace moved to the old-fashioned landline phone and lifted the handle.

"Sir?" a man's voice replied immediately.

"My records are on file," he said. "I'll need someone to deliver me spare clothing shortly. Probably Rowena as well, though she'll call you. For now, I need to make an outside call on a secured line. Please connect me and set your encryption in place."

"Stand by," the man replied "You will have a dial tone in three seconds."

Chace waited, then dialed Thane's number from memory. Thirteen hour time difference between Tokyo and DC. Not even midnight here. Late morning there.

"You have a serious problem on your hands," she said as soon as she answered.

"Could you narrow that down?" he asked. Not grumpy. Maybe a little sarcastic, but he'd been on the sharp end of the spear for the last few hours and didn't need Monday morning quarterbacking right now.

"Rowena Cai," Thane continued. "Chun-Bin Cai, to give you her proper, Cantonese name. Daughter of Yan-Li Cai. Our records are more compartmentalized than I had appreciated, and I've started the process of fixing that, but it won't help you tonight. Plus, it happened a long time ago, and nobody had the right flags in the computer system until I got your Quartz call."

"Who is Yan-Li Cai?" Chace asked.

That name seemed to be the important one. The one that had Thane in something of a lather, which was itself frightening.

"In 1988, you shot him in a Kowloon office building," Thane replied.

Chace went cold. Before he could respond, she continued.

"Not you, obviously," she said, "but one of your predecessors. At the time, we'd thought he was dead, because the man disappeared into the depths of the Hong Kong underground for nearly a decade before he emerged again. The Chace Haig who pulled the trigger was medically retired in 1993 after a mission gone bad and died in '96 from the lingering effects of his wounds. Has she broken your cover?"

Chace considered the last several days. Things she had said. Things he had mentioned.

"Not directly," he replied after several seconds. "However, she originally gave off the impression of looking for me. Of being a honeypot of some sort. Knowing who she works for, did someone else spot me and route her down?"

"Tell me about the ambush," Thane said, sidestepping the question.

Chace walked her through the entire evening, from leaving his hotel to landing at the safe house. She listened once, then had him repeat it while she started firing off questions.

Like him, her memory was almost photographic. Plus, she might have had access already to some of the cameras that must have witnessed the entire affair. Certainly, in London it would have been recorded from a dozen angles. More if they knew the restaurant was underworld connected.

After an hour, he was exhausted. Thane had folks in her office or on the call, because the questions had taken on other tones and focus as folks narrowed down everything.

"Where does that leave us?" he finally asked. "She's across the hallway, possibly asleep by now, or waiting for me to return to whatever this new mission calls for. She still has her phone, but I don't think she's willing to risk activating it until she's more confident of the situation. And that confidence comes from me. What do I tell her?"

"This is why you have a problem, Haig," Thane replied. "The man you beat up appears to be a Taiwanese Intelligence agent known on the streets as Dragon Scholar Zheng. Ru-Chen Zheng, specifically. The one you shot also belongs to Taiwanese Intelligence."

"Taiwanese Intelligence?" he clarified. "Why the hell are they launching assassinations against Chinese citizens in Tokyo?"

"We can't tell if this is a rogue op or not," she said. "I've had to reach up my chain of command pretty high, and someone is going to reach across for answers from Taipei, but that will take time. And they might tell us to get stuffed anyway, regardless of other relationships."

"Who is Rowena Cai?" he asked, circling back.

"The background you need will take too long, even after I have someone boil it all down into an executive summary," she told him. "And given that, we're talking possibly sixty to eighty pages of details."

"Shit," Chace muttered.

"Agreed," she acknowledged. "Near as we can tell, the British taking Hong Kong from the Qing government in 1841 triggered the formation of several underground nationalist movements. The kind dedicated to ousting all foreigners from China, which at the time included the Qing, because they originated in Manchuria. They were sheltered in Hong Kong from the Chinese government, from which they launched occasional assaults."

"The Boxer Rebellion in 1900?" he asked, digging deep into the bits and pieces of Chinese history he'd picked up at Yale.

"Likely connected," Thane agreed. "Plus several others. As I said at the top, the information I needed was too compartmentalized to be quickly accessed, so I have pulled rank on a few folks and demanded that analysts start reshaping our intelligence to take into account whatever the hell you've stumbled into."

"Do I evac Japan tomorrow?" Chace asked.

Seriously, that was the proper protocol in a situation like this. He had stashed spare identity papers that were issued by the US Government and would get him to Seattle or Paris easily enough. Disappear again?

"This is where things get tricky, Chace," she countered. "You might be in a position to gather more intelligence on certain elements of the Chinese underground that we're not currently privy to. To operate as long as they have, the Cai organization has to have all sorts of connections into the CCP at an extremely high level. Maybe the top, but certainly elements close to the Politburo and senior party officials who would normally be shaking them down or crushing them like Xi's been up to with a few folks over the last few years."

"Should I cultivate Rowena as a contact?" he continued, seeing the shape of the thing she was building.

"You are a criminal, Haig," Thane chuckled. "A man who finds things for people. Plus, we need to know if Yan-Li Cai has broken your cover by recognizing you somewhere. Not you you, but the identity of Chace Haig itself. Is your mission at risk sufficient that we need to consider killing Yan-Li Cai and destroying his organization? I can't answer that right now, and I have Assistant Deputy Secretaries arguing loudly with each other in secured rooms over who gets to issue you orders on this one."

"Should I go rogue for a while?" he asked, astonished at his own audacity.

Plus, this call was going to be recorded and analyzed at levels of security above the President, after the last one reminded everyone that you couldn't always trust the politicians who got elected.

"You are not going rogue, Chace," she countered sternly. "My orders to you at present involve exercising extreme care. At the same time, I'm pretty confident that all this noise is going to leak somewhere soon. The Chinese have definitely penetrated Japanese Intelligence systems, so we don't trust those entirely. And the Taiwanese are listening in, because the woman you are working with probably qualifies as an enemy of the KMT, if not the Taiwanese government itself. I know that you just arrived at a safe house, but I cannot determine how safe it is at this moment and won't until I can make some other calls to various people. Adjust your priorities accordingly."

Chace went cold, all over again.

It was one thing to be playing these sorts of dangerous games with criminals. They tended to be looking over their shoulders constantly for the authorities to send hit teams or fly bombs in through windows when they wanted to make a point.

He might be on the other side of things now. One of those folks that had to face that.

Or rather, it might get worse, because he'd already broken up one attempt on Rowena's life on a public street.

How pissed were the Taiwanese going to be at him, for having shot one of their people, even in self-defense? Had he just stepped across a line in their eyes?

Worse, if he'd also shot Rowena's father, regardless of the technicalities, was she his enemy? Obviously, in retrospect, the name had been a trigger. And Yan-Li had sent an agent to look, because Chace couldn't be the same guy, even as he had the same cover.

Nephew? Cousin? Even metaphorical son, if you wanted to revisit the sins of the fathers?

Utter, freaking mess.

And Thane was ordering him to vanish before the President or the Secretary of State could weigh in on ordering Chace Haig to assassinate someone. Like Rowena.

Well, shit.

"What questions do you have for me, Chace?" she asked in an oddly neutral tone after a long beat to digest that.

Like she knew someone else was listening. Possibly in the room with her. Someone that might not catch the subtleties of her vocabulary.

"None at the moment," he lied with all the facility of his job. "I'm going to take a long, hot shower, then crash for a while and sleep on it. After breakfast I'll call you directly for an update and you can update the situation for me."

"Understood, Chace," she said. "Talk to you in about eight hours."

She hung up and Chace put the phone down.

Thane had pretty much told him outright that he should consider this safe house already blown. And she was probably right.

He took a couple of minutes to focus, then grabbed his jacket and moved to the door.

CHAPTER
SEVENTEEN

Chace cracked the door and looked. Presumably, security would not be surprised to see him cross at some point, having put them so close initially, when they couldn't have been sure who Chace had been bringing.

Beautiful women brought certain assumptions to the table in this game. Especially outsiders drawn into a safe house.

He slid across and went ahead and opened her door. She'd left the invitation open, so he didn't figure it would be nice to make her get out of bed it he knocked just now.

And things had gotten deadly serious. Deadlier, maybe.

Opening the door, he found the front room lit by a lamp on the lowest setting, with the bedroom door open to darkness beyond.

Rowena's clothing was neatly stacked on the couch, in case he'd had any questions about where her mind had gone in the two hours he'd been on the phone with Thane. It was just a shame that he couldn't take her up on it.

Chace grabbed the stack as he went by and found her in the bedroom. The lights were down but not off, and her eyes glittered as she watched him approach.

He took a moment to put her clothes on the dresser then moved to the edge of the bed, stretching out atop the covers with his shoes still on.

Her hand reached out and he took it.

"Trouble?" Rowena asked carefully.

"Yes," he nodded, working out exactly how thin the ice was likely to get under his feet as he pursued this line of logic.

He'd given serious thought to vanishing. Leaving her here and letting the housekeeper take care of her for a few days.

Assuming the Taiwanese didn't arrive first ad take care of Rowena Cai in their own way.

Even Thane hadn't been sure how long they had, but if the Secretary of State was involved, the President himself was probably being briefed this afternoon, DC time.

As much as the man was an old-time pol turned grand statesman, Chace doubted that it would protect them if he saw a need to make a statement. Or send a message.

"I just got off the phone with some people," he told her, measuring lies and omissions and calculating the best way to lean into the latter as much as he could.

It might be possible to recruit her as a contact of some sort. Even if he had shot her father, once upon a time.

Sins of the fathers, and all that.

"And?" she asked, sitting up in a way that distracted him for a moment.

Everything had been covered previously, so he'd only had his imagination. It was even better in person.

"And they are pretty sure that the men who attacked us were Taiwanese Intelligence," Chace told her. "Possibly KMT, but they weren't sure, so they didn't know if it was a sanctioned operation or someone seeing a chance to do something stupid."

He watched her absorb and process that. Quickly. Not surprised.

That spoke volumes.

Rowena nodded.

"Are you Chinese Intelligence, Rowena?" he asked, mostly to take her down the wrong rabbit hole.

Obfuscation and deflection. Always.

"What? No," she countered sharply. "Why would you...oh, right, that actually makes sense."

"Why is the KMT sending assassins after you?" he asked, unrelenting now that he'd gotten her into motion.

Headed the wrong direction, but moving. And not asking him who his friends were. Not yet, anyway.

"Because the Civil War never ended," she replied carefully.

"That was almost seventy-five years ago," Chace said.

She nodded and held up a hand to pause him, unmindful of her naked beauty as she composed words.

He wondered how many of them would be lies.

"The Republic fell when those people fled to Taiwan," she said. "For the longest time, they harbored dreams of returning and retaking China, because Mao had gone insular and weak."

Chace nodded for her to continue.

"There's so much more," she shook her head. "The February 28th Incident. *Dang Guo*. How much modern Chinese history do you know?"

"Pitifully little, considering what I've fallen into," Chace admitted. "And while I would love to sit here and ogle you all night as you told me, we have trouble."

"How soon are they coming for us?" she asked. "For me?"

"I don't know," he admitted. "The people I talked to didn't know. I told them that I was going to take a long shower, sleep in, and call them in the morning to see if there was any useful news."

"You don't plan on being here in the morning, do you?" she nodded, seeing the shape of things that quickly.

"I have no dog in this fight," he nodded back. "Or didn't until some idiot stepped out of the crowd and tried to shoot me. Pretty sure I pissed them off, so now I have enemies on that side of the equation. At the same time, I dragged you here, and they are likely coming for us. We need to be gone."

"Do we tell the local resident?" she asked, throwing back the covers and sliding away from him.

Just as well. He really wanted to grab hold and drag her back. Enjoy one night with this amazing, beautiful woman before they were running for their lives.

But they were already running.

"I'll concoct a cover story," Chace replied, standing and watching her dress with quick precision.

Last night's clothes, because protocol would be to deliver new stuff in the morning, assuming the agents had gone to sleep.

Pants and a tunic top that belted. Stylish, and durable enough for what he needed. It was the shoes that might be a problem, and why he didn't just open the patio door and climb down to the ground below right now.

She'd worn heels. Not particularly tall ones, but crippling if you were trying to cross open terrain. And he would be.

She caught his glance and nodded.

"I can't run in those," she said, walking over to the heels.

"Leave them," he replied. "Back my bullshit story if necessary but otherwise keep mostly quiet and professional."

"Where are we going?" she asked as he moved to the door and into the front room.

"Away," Chace said. "We've got to run. And keep running, because I'm not sure who I can trust."

"If it was the KMT, then my people might be safe," she replied, catching up and catching his hand to stop him short of the door. "You asked me to trust you earlier, sight unseen. I'm asking the same of you."

"You never answered my question earlier, Rowena," he said. "Who are you? If you aren't CCP Intelligence, why does the KMT want you dead so badly that they would try something like this in Tokyo?"

She paused, calculations whirring in her eyes as she weighed his soul.

"I belong to an organization," she said slowly. "Not CCP, but we've traditionally supported them. More nationalist than communist, but fellow-travelers, to use the old Soviet vernacular. If we can get to them, they'll be able to protect us from the KMT."

"Maybe," he said bluntly. "But you came to Tokyo looking for me, didn't you? Me specifically. Why?"

"A case of mistaken identity," she replied. "Something happened a long time ago and you have a similar name to the person in question, so I was sent to investigate. You can't be him, but things got out of hand before I could learn more. Is that enough for you to trust me?"

"Am I walking into a trap?" he asked. "Someone else going to kill me to protect your secrets?"

• "Not if you can keep them secret," she said, which was at least as honest an answer as you normally got in his industry.

And one hell of an opening into her organization, if he could somehow skate across ice that thin.

But then, only two of his six predecessors had actually retired, both of them physically broken by the demands of the job. He'd know that going in.

And still agreed to all the plastic surgery and personal transformation necessary to become Chace Haig.

But he had his first answer. They remembered Chace Haig. And must have suspected something when a new one arrived, but hadn't been able to figure it out. They would shortly, whatever happened next.

Would they blow his cover entirely? Was he about to be outed and burned because of a mistake his predecessor had made a long time ago?

Normally, Chace Haig kept a lower profile. If you were a criminal just breaking into the bigger leagues from the neighborhood stuff, you didn't have connections, so maybe somebody shared his name and information.

Chace got introduced, did business with folks for a while, then everybody moved on when those same folks got their own organizations built up.

Assuming nobody tore them down in the meantime.

Then some other newcomer would come along, and need a name, and get introduced to Chace Haig.

Not always the same one. Always the same business.

He nodded.

"I guess I have to trust you, then," he said, committing himself into as deep a problem as she'd been willing to go with him.

He could walk safely right now. Could have. Slipped out and let someone take her out or arrest her, depending on who won the argument.

Clear the decks.

Except that the potential upside here was jarringly huge, and he needed to exploit it.

Even if it got risky.

"Now what?" she asked.

"Come with me," he told her, opening the out door.

Rowena walked on his flank. He was right-handed, so she walked on that side, where he would automatically block with his left.

Chace Haig was a spy. That much was obvious, if unspoken. And she doubted that he had been dangled as bait, because they would have prepared him better for running into her organization.

More and more, she began to believe that Father's overreaction had triggered a chain of consequences that she needed to escape. To get ahead of so she could step out of the way. Something.

He'd asked for her trust, and she'd given it. She'd asked for his, and he was correct to worry, if he didn't know who she worked for.

Or why people might take a dislike to a man named Chase Haig.

They descended the stairs and met the small Japanese woman house-keeper at the bottom.

"Is there a problem, Mr. Haig?" she asked in a polite tone, standing in such a way that someone with guns was watching from out of sight.

The woman appeared ready to throw herself flat if she needed to.

Chace walked right up to the woman and bowed in the proper, Japanese style. It also let him talk quietly.

"Someone in your organization leaked," he murmured, just barely loud enough for Rowena to hear. "At present, my superiors believe that outsiders have been given these coordinates and are *en route* with inimical intentions."

Rowena watched the woman turn almost white as she understood the implications.

"Quartz," she intoned, suddenly desperately, *massively* lethal for all her age and previous demeanor. "What do you need?"

It was like the chihuahua had turned into a werewolf in front of them. Rowena looked around for another ambush.

"She needs shoes capable of overland travel," Chace was saying. "Pistols with two magazines of reload each. What is the weather forecast?"

"Drying out and generally warming for a few days, last I checked," the woman replied. "Come with me."

Chace followed, Rowena on his heels as the woman led them deeper into the house.

Through a door, the architecture changed from polite and welcoming to industrial. A guard stood at a door down a hallway, perking up immediately on seeing them.

"Status?" he asked crisply.

"We need access to the armory," the housekeeper replied. "Condition Two."

Rowena noted that the man nodded, paling ever so slightly, then drew a keycard from a pocket and pressed it against a sensor that had been hidden behind him.

The door unlocked like a brick dropped from a window, thunking hard.

"Orders?" the guard asked, ignoring her and Chace to focus on the housekeeper.

"Our guests will arm and depart," she said. "Secure the perimeter before and after and stand by to potentially repel an assault."

"In motion," he said, stepping immediately past them and receding quickly.

Somewhere, Rowena heard a door open and close, but she was into the next room.

Armory. Five meters wide. Nine or so deep. Pistols. Submachine guns. Rifles. Heavier things that she found both fascinating and frightening to discover in a house in the Japanese countryside.

Someone was ready for a war here.

Chace Haig had to belong to someone's government. US? British?

French? He didn't have any of the subtle cues of Eastern Europe or Germany. Or Scandinavia.

She'd assume American until proven otherwise, in spite of the cues he did give off. She already knew that Chace Haig was a chameleon.

Chace moved to a wall with a series pistols hanging for immediate use and took one down.

"SIG P365?" he asked the woman.

"Base model," she nodded. "Ammunition and magazines in the drawers below it."

Chace nodded and turned. Rowena felt his gaze settle on her like some terrible monster.

"How good are you with pistols?" he asked simply.

"Good enough," she replied.

"Preference?" he asked, turning back to the wall. "I prefer the SIG. This is a combat model that stacks ten rounds and conceals well. With your tunic, a shoulder holster wouldn't work, but we can put a belt carrier underneath."

"9mm is good," Rowena said. "Another like that lets us share magazines if we need to."

She caught that hint of approval in his eyes, that she should automatically know such things, but they were both in the same business, regardless of who they worked for.

He popped the magazine out and the slide open before handing it to her, then grabbed one for himself.

"Holsters?" he asked.

"Here," the housekeeper pulled a drawer open.

Quickly, they got ready, his in a shoulder holster that disappeared under that jacket in ways she hadn't appreciated before. Hers went back on her kidney where it was hard to see and uncomfortable.

"We'll need to change you into something else," the woman announced. "This way."

The next room was a laundry, with a closet of things. The housekeeper studied her closely then pulled a jacket, handing it to her along with another shoulder holster like Chace's. Dark gray hiking shoes from a box along with socks.

"Electronics?" the housekeeper asked.

"None we'd trust at present," he replied to her nod. "And we have cash sufficient for now."

"Very good," the woman bowed. "This way to the rear entrance."

Rowena was surprised to got down two long flights of stairs, lights coming on via sensors as they did. The stairs were welded steel. The walls raw concrete. The air a little stale.

She led them to a door with a massive bar that set deep into staples. A button opened it and the woman opened it on silent hinges.

"One hundred and seventy-three meters," she explained. "You come out into the side of a different drainage culvert that takes you another forty-six meters before emerging into a ravine. From the ravine, head downstream to end up on the outskirts of Tokyo again, or upstream to get into the highlands. You'll need this."

She produced a flashlight and handed it to Chace before stepping back and bowing.

"My profuse apologies at the failure of my organization, Mr. Haig," she said severely.

"We're not sure the leak was inside the house," Chace replied carefully. "It may have been electronic eavesdropping on the communications lines. Those are known to have been compromised from time to time."

"Nevertheless, we will hold this facility against attacks, giving you time to evade," she said. "Give them hell."

"I intend to," he said.

Rowena stepped to the side as the big door began to close. Bank vaults would be jealous of that solidity.

For a moment, they were in darkness, then Chace turned on the light and shined it up so she could see his face.

"Ready?" Chace asked.

"Let's do this," Rowena replied.

Chace turned and studied the corridor. Made of three-meter concrete pipe, but dry. Nothing indicating lights or power, so just another drain from somewhere if you didn't know where you were going.

He shined it forward and moved, Rowena falling in behind him. He'd asked for her trust and gotten it. Shortly, he'd have to trust her, though he didn't know when that would change.

They needed to get away from her phone, if only because competent spies would have been waiting for it to appear on the cellular network. In Southwest Asia, that was frequently the way US forces targeted someone for bombs.

Chace didn't think that anyone would get that crazy in Japan, but he also wasn't willing to trust them.

Forward. Long walk.

They came out at a grate like a jail cell, vertical bars intended to keep animals out, with a few side drains that had flowed in and underneath the door.

It wasn't locked, but required a human to open. Did Japan have raccoons? He honestly didn't know, and it wasn't worth asking.

Rowena was close. Chace went ahead and drew the SIG, just because that door would make noise. She did the same a moment later.

Opening it, he stepped through and down about thirty centimeters.

Enough to keep water from flowing back this way, even though the pipe was slightly inclined.

Hidden, because this was the back way to escape the safe house in an emergency.

Like now.

How soon would someone show up and knock? Or try to kick the front door in, depending on who it was? And how well could they hold? It had been a Quartz call that started all this, so Chace was willing to believe that they could stop anybody trying, especially if they were alerted to the attempt.

He just needed to get as far away from the place as he could.

He shined the light uphill into the new tunnel, watching it fade with distance. Almost worth slipping up there and hiding, but he had no idea what it might be connected to.

"Worth considering?" Rowena asked.

"I prefer freedom to maneuver," he replied.

"Where are we going?" she asked.

"No clue at present," Chace shrugged. "Not my neighborhood to know who to talk to. That's where I'll rely on you."

He watched the gleam come into her eyes, even as dim as the tunnel was.

She'd be in charge. Would she shoot him, then call her people in to rescue her? Capture him and haul him off somewhere to be interrogated or tortured by her father's people?

Or could he trust her?

Hell of a way to find out.

Chace turned downhill and moved. The complete darkness gave way to a lighter circle in the distance.

"I'm turning the light out," he warned her, then did.

Her hand came up and touched his hip so he could know where she was.

Another forty meters, and he could see the end of the culvert. See where it flattened out onto a slab, then fell away, presumably into a ditch or creek.

Then what? He'd burn that bridge when he got there, assuming nobody was camped on a nearby ridge with a nightscope and a rifle. Waiting.

Chace drew a breath at the cusp and stuck his head out enough to look around.

Heavy brush above, which would cut down sight lines. Darkness below. Some moon, but he hadn't been paying attention, save that the cloud earlier had blown through, leaving stars.

Not cold, but cooling some.

"Here goes nothing," he murmured to Rowena as he stepped out and let his nightvision take it all in.

Nobody shot him, which was a plus. He gestured her to join him, and they looked around.

"Tokyo or the hills?" she whispered.

"This just became your op," he replied. "I can survive for a few days rough easily, but I would stand out enough to draw attention when I came back, unless I walked up to the front door of the safe house and knocked. Or called more friends."

"Quartz," she nodded in the moonlight, looking even more beautiful than she had over dinner. "You could always have them rescue you in a few days."

"I dislike being hunted," Chace told her. "Chafes me. Makes me grumpy enough that next time I don't shoot the bastard in the leg to disable him."

"You willing to trust me?" she asked, still dancing around that topic.

Agent for an unknown organization. At least to Chace. Thane seemed to know more, but hadn't been able to fully brief him.

Not with all the other ears listening in to that call. That had been the subtext.

"Yes," Chace replied simply, hearing her slight catch of breath.

Not a gasp, but headed in that direction.

Just like that.

But he had to trust her or burn her, and they had come to the decision point.

"Let's get to the edges of Tokyo, then," she said. "I can look around and find us a place to lie low. Not a safe house, but a house that should be safe."

"You leading or am I?" he asked. "How's your fieldcraft?"

"Adequate, but not expert," she admitted. "Yours?"

"I'll lead, then," Chace nodded. "You keep me headed in the right direction."

"I will, Chace," she said.

Not much to do from there. He was committed.

Chace found a game trail down to the water and started to follow what was largely a dry creek bed, down into the city.

Rowena marveled at how quietly Chace moved through the brush. How smoothly and carefully he placed each step, without appearing to.

Who had trained him?

She'd spent some time around military veterans from several countries. He didn't move like a soldier. They had a particular walk. A way they held their shoulders when expecting trouble.

No, Chace was merely a spy. American, most likely.

Not the man who had shot her father, but somehow connected? Would it be safe to bring Chace in with her? Or would she need to make sure that he got away at the last instant and was able to disappear when her own folks came to rescue her?

She'd asked for his trust. Was she willing to burn him, having gotten it?

Too much to weigh, and she didn't need to do anything yet, as there was no way in hell she was turning her phone on again until she could be certain she was safe.

They'd need another burner, like Chace had bought before. And she knew he had enough cash on hand, unlike her, so she'd be relying on the man to get her out of this situation, even as he was relying on her.

Partners? At least for a time?

She could work with that.

They came around a bend in the creek bed and she could see lights ahead.

Japan as a culture was slowly dying. Population pressures had collapsed, and numbers were in freefall. There were entire villages where only the elderly remained. Or perhaps grandchildren as well, with their parents off in one of the cities trying to make a living.

China faced something similar, perhaps a generation from now, because women like her weren't immediately giving up their dreams to start families, and the men didn't understand why they might support a woman's art. India had another generation after that if they were lucky.

It was a shame she couldn't convince Chace to join her. Partners, at least for a few days?

She didn't have any interest in retiring and returning to the legitimate family business. Would he?

Rowena smiled where Chace couldn't see it and followed him.

"Village up ahead," he muttered, pausing. "Possibly dogs."

She nodded.

"Let's get close, then we can see what kind of place it is," she told him.

Hopefully, one of those older villages where Tokyo had almost expanded far enough to engulf it. A small town, instead of a suburb of empty houses and old people where they would stick out.

She had a few friends in Japan she might call, but nothing like saying Quartz into a phone and getting instant armed concierge service like Chace had.

Then she heard the sound of a highway. Or something. A busy roadway, in spite of it being after midnight, rather than those tiny lanes that you got when you were too far removed from urban civilization.

"Circle up and out to your right," she instructed Chace. "I want to see the highway."

"There's a bridge up there," he replied.

"Excellent," Rowena decided. "Maybe we'll get lucky and find a restaurant or hotel that won't ask too many questions."

She still had one hand on his hip, so she felt his shrug, then he was off.

They climbed up out of the gully and along a path that felt like something the locals kept up. Then a sidewalk of sorts.

The road, when they got close, was a good sign. Cars moving along nicely.

Rowena caught his hand and pulled him short. They'd hidden the pistols once they'd been certain that they were away, but she had a plan.

"Let me inspect you," she ordered, moving to brush off a few leaves and things that had accumulated, as well as running her hand through his wavy hair once to smooth it out. "How do I look?"

He did the same, touching her delicately and carefully as they got a little presentable.

"Out on the road, I'm going to pretend to be Japanese, and tell folks you don't speak hardly anything except French, okay?" she asked.

"*Oui*," he replied.

She smiled. He wasn't all that fluent, but she'd heard him say a few things. Better than a tourist, but hiding was good.

She took his hand and led him to the downhill side of the road. As Chace had said earlier, sometimes you just bullshit things and leave out a lot of details that might trip you up later.

The road went through the village, and she could see other bridges where the creek wound its way back and forth. Lights on outside, but none of the houses seemed awake, and no shops or such that they could get assistance. No dogs woke and challenged them.

Just as well, she didn't want to leave any memory of passing this way, in spite of being several kilometers from the safe house, over and around.

They got up to the verge of the road and started walking. Rowena waved at cars passing. Eventually, one slowed down, then stopped next to them and the window came down.

"Problems?" the man driving asked.

"Our car broke down up there," she gestured towards the hills above. "We were walking to find someplace where we could call for help. Could you drop us in town?"

She smiled, looking innocent. More importantly, presenting as upper middle class in ways that didn't immediately make her look dangerous.

Two lost souls, out walking in the middle of the night, because something had gone wrong.

The man studied her. Studied Chace in his nicer jacket and friendly smile.

She heard the doors unlock.

"Hop in," the man said. "I'm going as far as Ome. Will that work?"

"That would be excellent," she replied, reaching for the door and opening it. "Thank you. We can get what we need there."

"Good," the man said as they both got in back. "Hate to see strangers walking. Your husband, he is American?"

"He is French," Rowena replied. "And doesn't speak much Japanese. We were on a trip to visit my family in Tokyo, and decided to see some of the countryside when the rental conked out."

"Terrible, that," he nodded. "Let's get you to town."

And they were off. She snuggled up against Chace in her role as his spouse, at least in the eyes of the driver. Middle-aged male. Balding and heavy, but smiling and friendly.

They made small talk as he drove down into the outskirts of Tokyo, Rowena inventing a whole life on the fly to distract the man, if he was somehow asked about it later.

Nothing that could be traced to her, especially if he thought her to be Japanese. Hard to distinguish in the darkness.

He came to rest at an intersection with an all-night noodle house on one corner, a bodega on another, and a gas station.

"This would be perfect," Rowena said. "We'll exit here and offer blessings on your house for your help."

"Are you certain?" he asked, but she had already nudged Chace into motion and both of them got up onto the sidewalk quickly.

"Thank you, again," she told the man, and watched him wave and drive away as they started towards the noodle shop.

She wasn't hungry, but they needed time to plan their next steps, and how to get to safety.

Chace followed her across the street to a shop with music playing when they opened the door and stepped in.

Wood and bamboo paneling. Old. Grungy. Cigarette smoke stuck to the walls and filled the air.

She signaled to the bartender, or whatever his title was, and moved to a booth as far from everyone else as she could get. Not a lot of people here, about half and half folks still up after a late night of partying and those up extremely early to catch a train into Tokyo proper.

They stood out, but not as bad. And weren't walking the streets right now where they might be seen by a curious police officer. Or an assassin. There couldn't be that many ways down out of the hills, if the folks went looking.

"We need to get someplace quiet," he told her as they sat.

She nodded, but remained quiet as the bartender came over and studied them.

He didn't speak Japanese fast enough to keep up with Rowena, but the man seemed to accept what she told him, grunting as he withdrew.

"Tea coming, and noodles," she finally said. "How long until sunrise?"

"Couple of hours," he nodded. "Sleep would be good."

"How do you feel about a coffin at the train station?" she grinned. "Those will be empty during the day and clean."

"Hardly the place to fool around," he grinned back. "At least as I remember such things."

"Safer than a hotel tonight," she nodded. "Today. Whatever we call it. The sun will be up soon and we can hide for a time."

"Your phone safe?" he asked.

"Unlikely," she shook her head sourly. "Possibly not until I get back to Hong Kong. Like last night, we'll need to get a burner, but it's more tricky here."

"Worth heading deeper into Tokyo to hide?" he asked.

This was where he'd have to trust her. And play it on her terms. If she had an organization around here, she could vanish into it, like he'd been planning to do last night.

Or he could trust his luck that she wasn't an elaborate trap, a black widow luring him in.

"I think food and a nap would be good," she replied. "The heat will die down at some point and maybe we can hunt them instead."

"You think that's wise?" Chace asked, watching her emotions play out.

Anger. Exhaustion. Stubbornness.

Reminded him of someone.

"I don't like getting shot at," she murmured. "Especially by those damned Manchu who think they are superior to the rest of us. They could have left me alone, so they don't get to complain if I don't return that favor."

Hot. He understood. Chace hated it, too.

Worse, the Taiwanese were nominally US allies, though this wasn't his sphere of operations. Her organization, according to her and bits he'd gotten from Thane, was a Chinese nationalist, rather than merely communist. Older than the Party by a century.

Patriot, and he wasn't going to argue with her that she was wrong, because he did know a little bit about how China had come to be where they were in the twenty-first century.

And maybe he owed those punks a few as well, especially if they were still hunting him and Rowena.

The bartender returned with a teapot and mugs, plus two bowls of udon in broth.

Chace hadn't realized how hungry he was until he smelled that, but he'd had dinner some eight hours ago, and been on the run since then.

They grunted thanks to the man and dug in.

It was going to be a long day ahead.

CHAPTER
TWENTY-TWO

Ru-Chen looked up as the door opened and Manager Kwok entered the examination room.

"Good news, Dragon Scholar," the man said in a quiet voice.

They were alone, but the doctor had just left.

"Sir?" Ru-Chen asked.

"We have tracked down Cai Chun-Bin," Kwok replied. "Or rather, the man she was with turns out to be far more than we originally understood him to be."

"Far more dangerous, yes," Ru-Chen said.

"Indeed, Dragon Scholar," Kwok nodded. "Fortunately, Kuei-Ho's wound was not bad, as the banker shot him in the leg. He will make a full recovery, once he is released from police custody in the hospital and flown to Taipei. How is your head?"

"Mild concussion, sir," Ru-Chen acknowledged. "The doctor gave me something and it is already receding. My apologies for letting the man best me and the woman get away."

"You could not know who he was," Kwok nodded. "I have been in contact with several people in Taipei and this Haig turns out to be one of those underworld fences, as noted, but he has a much wider and deeper scope of activities than we originally understood. He has dealt with most of the criminals in Europe and the Middle East at one time or another. Dangerous people. Enemies of the state. As is he."

"Sir?" Ru-Chen pressed, hopeful.

"When you get out of the here in a few minutes, I want you to take charge of the search for this Chace Haig and Cai Chun-Bin," Manager Kwok said. "We have tracked them to a safe house in the hills west of Tokyo, but reports indicate that they may have subsequently fled. They can't have gone far, because we're watching the airports."

"Still in Tokyo, then?" Ru-Chen asked. "Or gone upcountry to hide?"

"If the latter, we're unlikely to find them before they can escape you," Manager Kwok nodded. "You assume that they are still local and try to flush them out. If nothing else, it will show us where Cai's organization has people embedded, so we can remove them. Taipei is not being kept in the loop on this operation. You will have autonomy, reporting to me. Am I clear?"

Ru-Chen smiled in spite of the fading headache. That American had embarrassed him. Knocked him down and taken his own weapon to shoot Kuei-Ho, then escape.

There would be debts to settle over this. And the look in Manager Kwok's eyes promised that Haig and Cai would be the ones paying.

"You are very clear, sir," Ru-Chen asked. "When can I start?"

"As soon as the doctor discharges you."

TWENTY-THREE

Thane studied the man seated across the conference room table from her. He studied her back.

They didn't do names, even at the center of a secured facility. Not even really ranks. Both of them existed inside the US Department of the Treasury, because that had been the easiest way to stay away from those bozos at Homeland Security a generation ago when that Department had been formed, absorbing so many agencies and bureaus to turn into the beast inside the Intelligence and Law Enforcement apparatus.

Above the two of them on the org charts were only politicians. Folks with titles like Assistant Secretary for something or other. People who got personally approved by the Senate, stayed for a while, then left.

Certain operations needed to be shielded, even from them.

This man was one of the top career bureaucrats in the Office of Terrorism and Financial Intelligence. Frequently, the exact man who read certain reports she produced, based on things Chace Haig was doing in the field. Before he passed anonymous bits up to his superiors.

Or not.

"We could call the Taiwanese off," he ventured, reaching for his coffee and taking a sip.

"Not without them asking a lot of questions and learning more than they should," Thane growled. "I've been running this op for more than a decade. Chace Haig has been in the field since 1962. I don't need whispers getting out that he's one of us. Even hints ruin everything we've built."

"And if the KMT kills him?" the man asked.

"Then I'll need about a year to finish training his replacement," Thane snapped. "Assuming that the politicians don't fuck this up so badly that we have to start over with a new name, a new legend, and rebuild everything from scratch."

"Would that be bad?" he asked. "The original agent existed in an era when telegraphs were the best way to communicate. Today, I can call someone in Tokyo or Taipei on my cell phone and talk to them. Is Chace Haig an anachronism?"

"He's the single best source of Human Intelligence you have," Than reminded the man. "Him and a handful of others, all created when it became clear that we could successfully infiltrate the shadows this way. Do you want to destroy all that? Because if you tell the Taiwanese, they are going to start wondering if some of the folks who do similar work in their neighborhood might be more than they seem. How quickly might we lose all of our assets in the underworld then?"

"They are mad enough to kill him," he said bluntly.

"Yes," she agreed. "And he took out three of them without any preparation or warning. And didn't kill them. If they try again, I suspect that Haig will escalate to lethal force. They better bring a lot of friends. Once he gets out, I'll make sure he stays out of Asia for a while. This was supposed to be his vacation out of his normal op zone, where he could relax."

"Best laid plans," he nodded, grinning and sipping his coffee.

Not that she could blame the man. Things had gone astray, but she'd kept Chace into play to infiltrate Cai's organization instead of extracting him safely. If he could.

They might also kill him, but if the KMT was sending assassins, and letting everyone know how angry they were, it would actually help his legend with the Mainlanders.

Later, Chace might be in a position to finish the job his predecessor had started thirty-five years ago. Timely, when the politicians were almost universally reviling the Chinese these days, even as about half of them sounded like Russian stooges when they got on the news.

"Chace is a big boy," Thane said. "He'll be fine, as long as nobody else gets involved and tries to mess with whatever status quo is in play right now. I'd rather not blow his cover by overtly extracting him, any more than he did with the girl, placing a Quartz call that turned around and blew up in our faces when our own allies were the shooters."

"What do you need me to tell the Assistant Secretary?" he asked.

"Nothing," Thane said. "That one of our operations got tangled up with a Taiwanese one, and we're trying to back away, if someone presses you into a corner. Chace didn't start it, but he will finish it if they act the fool. If you really wanted to be a shit, leak to Japanese Intelligence that the KMT is running a rogue assassination team in Tokyo and see how quickly someone drops a boom on them. That's probably all Chace needs to make his own escape. Just enough confusion."

"Understood," the man said, rising now. "I can run that level of bureaucratic interference easily enough. You keep me posted when your boy gets clear. Or killed. We can't do or say anything, but it gives me enough time to blunt whatever stupidity comes down from the Secretary and his Chief of Staff."

"Will do," Thane nodded. "And thank you."

"You've covered my ass enough times," he grinned as he got to the door. "At least here I get to return the favor."

Then she was alone. Thane let herself have a good grumble at the whole thing, mostly because one of her own predecessors had filed all the information the wrong way for what she needed today, or she might have better prepped Chace for traveling to Tokyo.

But even then, it had been a crap shoot somewhere. A face recognized. Maybe a name.

A ghost, given Yan-Li Cai's reaction.

Worst? She wasn't even sure if they needed to destroy Cai's organization at this point, regardless of what the politicians said.

Could she get Chace deep it enough to turn the whole thing inside out?

Chace held her hand and they walked like they were on a date, even as the sun would be coming up soon.

Good date, then.

She was walking him towards the train station, along with a few folks already in motion, presumably headed deep into the core of Tokyo to start their day. International finance and markets never slept these days, though Tokyo was largely the beginning of the cycle, unless something bad had happened in New York.

Still, they stood out against the wave of folks in dark suits and thin ties, anachronistic briefcase in one hand, making their way to town in the early morning hours.

Chace kept his head surreptitiously on a swivel, watching for trouble and listening to the night sounds that might presage the next attack. His great fear was that the KMT team would just go ahead and use a rifle next time. Sit up on a roof ledge where they would be impossible to detect. Fire a single shot that killed either her or him before there was any warning.

All the more reason to get under cover before daylight made the game easier for his foes.

The tide of bodies swept them up the stairs and into the building, but Rowena pulled him quickly to one side, into an eddy, as it were, then nodded to a corner.

Sleeper pods. Generally referred to as coffins everywhere else, because the original ones hadn't been much bigger, back in the eighties when they'd first grown popular.

Japanese business was still addicted to the concept of working long hours, then going out drinking with the boss, a system that rewarded the extroverts and punished the introverts, artists, and those folks that actually liked their wives, rare as that might be in a culture that still married for financial and social benefit.

Salarymen who got too drunk to make it home safely could crawl into one of the tiny rooms and sleep it off, going into the office and presumably changing into a clean suit they kept there for just that reason.

More recently, things had expanded. He saw a sign indicating a wing for single females to stay, away from the predators that roamed Tokyo's subway systems.

"I need cash," Rowena said, turning and leaning into him like they were a little drunk.

Chace pulled a wad of bills out and handed them to her. He could always place a call and get the location of a drop for more if he needed, since he wasn't about to use a card that could be traced.

Or instantly located if someone hacked the right system.

"You stay here," she nodded, turning and walking to a woman watching the space with eagle eyes.

Chase had no idea if a hotel or even a roadside motel would have been safer, but this would let them hide, and put them in a position to get into town later with a minimum of visibility.

Rowena approached the woman and drew her into a quiet conversation. At one point, the guardian perked up and looked over Rowena's shoulder, studying him hard. He had no idea what story Rowena was telling her, but it must have been good, because she nodded to herself and ignored him again.

Rowena subtly waved him closer and Chace joined them.

The guardian had been behind a desk. She rose now and lead them through a door into the hallway for women. Instead of Japanese business drunks.

Six spaces, all wider than Chace was expecting. Perhaps a queen-sized bed instead of the single that the men got. The doors rolled up like in a garage. All of them were currently empty. Nice, too. Two pillows. Lights. Plugs for equipment. Presumably a communal bathroom and shower somewhere, again isolated from the men.

"In," the woman said in Japanese.

He followed Rowena and they were inside. Rowena dropped the screen and locked it, then sighed audibly.

"She's expecting us to fool around for a while, then leave by lunch," Rowena said simply. "Her replacement takes over after that, and it would be easier not to explain anything."

"Nap and run?" he asked, turning to sit on the bed and slip his shoes off.

While hadn't planned on the sort of evening he'd faced, Weland and Thane had made sure that all his gear was multi-functional for those sorts of things. That included surprise cross-country hikes in the woods.

"Yes," Rowena agreed, dropping beside him to remove her own shoes. "Too bad we can't take advantage of the space, but I think we need sleep more than anything."

"Agreed," Chace grinned. "Maybe a rain check?"

"I'd like that," she offered.

He stripped his jacket and holster, placing the SIG where he could get to it in a hurry if someone opened the screen from the outside. She nodded and did the same, grinning as she stretched out on the bed.

For a moment, he considered joining her, but Chace had no idea how noisy they might get, nor how sound-proofed the walls were. No need to get into trouble.

He sat on the bed and crossed his legs, shifting so he could lean back.

"Not sleeping?" she asked, watching.

"Meditating," he replied. "Almost as good and I won't get as deep. Not that I think our friend will sell us out, but I won't feel comfortable until we get someplace where somebody's friends surround us."

"Mine?" she asked, turning a little serious, even as she distracted him with those hard curves.

"Can't really trust mine for a few days," he nodded. "The word was that someone somewhere in the chain passed along a message, telling the bad guys where we were. Until somebody cleans house, I'm out in the cold."

"I could bring you in from the cold," she teased.

"You could," he nodded. "What about your people? Will they object to sheltering both of us? Would you be safer if we split up?"

"You stick out around here, Chace," she reminded him, not that he needed reminding. "I can cover for you for a time. There will be questions later, but if your organization isn't directly my enemy, we can come to an accommodation."

"My only enemies in his hemisphere today operate out of Taipei," Chace said distinctly. "I was on vacation, until a beautiful woman walked up and introduced herself."

"So it's all my fault?" she grinned. "All the more reason to take care of you. Get you someplace safe."

"Safe is relative," Chace offered. "I still owe a few folks for ruining my night. Things had been going rather exceptionally, right up until the point I had to shoot that bozo."

"Rain check," she grinned. "I'm planning on cashing it in at some point."

"So you sleep for now," he nodded. "I'll focus and relax, then we can get some coffee or something strong when we get onto a mid-morning train. Those should be safer, yes?"

"Yes, but that also worries me," Rowena turned serious. "The morning rush will be a great place to hide. Later in the day, the trains won't be as crowded, but we don't know what they look like, if someone causes trouble."

"I'm planning to kill the next asshole who pulls a knife or gun on me, Rowena," Chace stated bluntly. "No warning. No other provocation. Drop them and move on to their buddies. I've got more friends I can call if I need to be smuggled out of Tokyo. I just don't know how many of them might want a bigger bribe not to turn me over to the Taiwanese."

She watched with dark, sober eyes. Measuring eyes. A nod.

"Who do you work for?" she asked, equally blunt.

"A Swiss bank that operates exactly within the precise limits of Swiss law," he replied, using his tones to suggest how close to over the lines with everyone else that might be. "Things even most German banks won't touch. A lot of Russian tycoons looking to launder money. A few African folks making European bribes disappear. Not a lot of Asian money in my Rolodex, but that's because I rarely make it this far east."

He left it at that. Chace Haig the international criminal banker had exactly that cover. Who that previous guy might have been could be any of a number of things, and Chace wasn't looking forward to meeting her father.

Worse than showing up to take her to prom, as it were.

She absorbed all that mutely, watching him for clues. Signs of lies, or whatever, but he'd lived this life for years among folks who would shoot him for weaker reasons. Mad dogs or paranoid fools.

"What about you?" he countered. "You've mentioned the Civil War, but that's Beijing and you said Hong Kong."

"Smuggling," she said, not sitting up but curled over to look at him square. "Whatever. Whoever. Wherever you need. Hong Kong has been the center of that action since it was founded. We still do that, but at the core, the Qing were invaders just like the Brits. Or the Russians. Or any of a number of other folks."

Chace nodded and they lapsed into silence. They had established a common ground upon which they could work. If he hadn't shot her father thirty-five years ago, even before he'd been born, she might be a fantastic contact into yet another organization that the US Government would like to keep tabs on.

Not something he was willing to trust today.

"Let's get someplace safe, then," he told her. "Inside a shell with your people protecting us until we can go after the bad guys."

"We could just escape," she reminded him.

"And they could have left me alone to a fantastic night with a beautiful woman intent on seducing me," he nodded. "Since they fucked that up, I intend to make them pay for it. Maybe next time, they'll mind their manners."

She nodded and let it go, closing her eyes.

Chace watched her breathe for a time, appreciating all that he'd seen and missed out on.

So much for his vacation.

He was back on the clock now.

TWENTY-FIVE

Chace had a timer in his head, counting. He opened his eyes and checked his watch, only being a few minutes ahead of it.

Ninety minutes had passed. He'd gone to the edge of darkness and hovered. She purred like a kitten when she snored. He considered reaching out and touching her, but wasn't sure how she woke.

"Rowena, it's time to wake up," he said.

She stirred. Breathed. Eyes opened.

"Not even a kiss?" she teased.

He leaned over to accommodate, absorbing some of her essence as he did. They lingered. It was a nice first kiss, but he didn't dare let himself get distracted. Not by this woman. Not while being hunted.

Or trying to insert himself sideways into her organization for Thane and the Institute. While not getting himself killed in the process.

He pulled back and slid off the edge of the bed to pull his holster back one and reset everything.

A man who has just had a fantastic nap and is ready to take on the world.

Close enough.

She joined him after a moment.

Rested, almost back to where they might have been last night, had things not gone entirely sideways.

She moved to the door and opened it. They stepped out and walked down the corridor and out into the larger area like two strangers that had gotten lost.

The guardian was the same woman. She grinned at Chace as they walked by. He grinned back, like they'd pulled one over on someone.

They had, but this woman didn't need to know who.

He had noted the schedule earlier. They moved to the kiosk and bought tickets for the next train into Tokyo, timing it just right to walk over and board the right car just as it was about to head out.

He hadn't seen anything, but there were enough folks around that any trouble would be loud and messy.

How badly did they want another shot at Rowena? Or him?

Chace didn't know.

Instead, they moved to a quiet corner and used bodies of other travelers to hide.

Quickly, the doors closed and the train started to roll.

Next stop, Tokyo.

TWENTY-SIX

Yan-Li looked up at the knock. It had been a long night. He'd supplemented with extra tea, but his humor was on edge. Ragged and jagged.

"Come!" he yelled.

The door opened and Guantin, Fu-Guo entered, a folder in one hand.

"Well?" Yan-Li growled at the man.

"Chun-Bin has vanished, sir," Guanting half-bowed. "We have been unable to located any trace of her from the moment she and the banker disappeared. However, there is news on the assassins."

Yan-Li perked up. Everything had been bad up until now. Shots fired. Daughter and stranger disappeared, with nothing to show for it.

At least this stranger wasn't the man who had shot him, even if they shared a name. Not a common one, as he understood Westerners, but nothing could be ignored right now.

"Speak," he ordered.

"Taipei," Guanting nodded. "Other contacts have confirmed the two men sent to the hospital as Taiwanese Intelligence agents. One was arrested, then someone made a call and they will transport him home by private plane. The other was treated and released into the custody of someone known to belong to a local KMT cell, according to our records."

"And?" Yan-Li pressed.

"And we are attempting to maintain surveillance on them, now that they have emerged, sir," Guanting replied. "Where should we prioritize our efforts?"

"The injured one did not immediately depart?" Yan-Li asked.

"Correct, sir," Guanting nodded.

"As there has been no contact with Chun-Bin, focus on the Republicans," he ordered. "If they have captured her, find her. If they haven't, then have people standing by to bring her in, or rescue her, as the situation warrants."

"Do we burn cover identities in Japan?" Guanting asked, careful now.

Yan-Li considered his options. Some of those folks had been in place for decades, quietly passing along tidbits of information occasionally, either for money or patriotism. Bringing them into the sunlight risked his enemies discovering how riddled some of their operations were.

At the same time, he needed to get his daughter back to safety. None of her siblings would be as prepared to eventually take over things after him, though he could force it upon them.

And there was Chace Haig, who shared the name of the man who had nearly killed him.

"Quite possibly," Yan-Li replied after a moment of thought. "I need to know who these newcomers are. Find that. Found out where they come from and how they knew where to find her. If there is someone in our organization leaking, I want that person found."

"And then?" Guanting asked, nervous.

"I will decide that if and when we find them," Yan-Li replied. "But find them. And have teams ready to strike in Tokyo, as soon as we know where to go. Mercenaries are preferable, to keep things at a distance, but do not hesitate to use our own people if we have to. We can always lean on cadre in Beijing to get them freed later, if that becomes necessary."

"I will see it it immediately, sir," he said, and then departed.

Yan-Li went back to reviewing the file in front of him. The full scenario that had eventually allowed to open China to the west, for good or ill.

And gotten him shot in the process.

Rowena watched people on the train. Chace stood out, but looked like a wealthy foreigner. They'd grabbed masks in the station and wore them now, as did everyone else, so it would be harder to identify her.

Chace was difficult to miss.

Fortunately, most of the folks on the train were women and younger people. Headed into Tokyo to shop at this time of day, perhaps, or have a day off. Few businessmen.

She stayed close to Chase. Not snuggled up where they might get in each others way if it came to drawing and shooting, but together.

The train ran quickly inwards, and they got off, transferring to the Chuo Main Line. As much as she wanted to go all the way downtown, to the places she really knew, Rowena had to assume that her enemies would be watching her friends.

Or had the assassins found her through Chace? If he was a spy, as she suspected, he would have filed a report about her, as she hadn't gone to great pains to conceal her identity, mostly to see how he would react to her last name. If his organization had leaked, was hers safe?

First, she needed to get into town, where she had more maneuvering space. Then a phone to check in and see what her father knew.

Then she could hunt.

And proper sleep at some point. She had catnapped last night while waiting for Chace, then this morning in the pod. He had to be running out of energy. Or at least getting a little dull in his reflexes.

That would never do.

Eventually, they were out on the surface streets. Mid-day. Pedestrians everywhere. She watched without looking like she was watching, turning random corners and doubling back. Dropping into shops to see who followed. Twice slipping out the back.

Nobody had found them, it seemed.

Theoretical tails lost, she found another kiosk selling cheap phones. Chace had given her money earlier. It got her a new device. Crappy and cheap, probably manufactured in Guangdong like most of them were these days.

She only needed it, like Chace had, for a short period.

They withdrew to an ice cream parlor done European style. Presumably preying on tourists, but she'd enjoyed her time in LA and still missed some of those things here. And sorbet would help with cold and fluids, when it promised to be hot later today.

She'd prefer to be inside with air conditioning before then.

Nobody followed them in. They ate in peace, then went out the back and into an alley.

Chace transitioned into a killing machine as she pulled out the phone, ignoring her to spot anyone approaching. That warmed her as she dialed.

"Hinton Holdings," a man answered quickly.

Rowena switched to Cantonese to reply. All dialects of Chinese used a single written form, but the accents were frequently so thick as to be impassible. Worse than someone from deep Appalachia talking to someone from the Bronx.

"There has been a problem with the delivery of my shipment," Rowena replied. "I need to speak with your manager."

"What was the ticket number, please?" he asked, suddenly paying much closer attention as she spoke.

Rowena fed him a numeric sequence, hearing him type it.

"Could you confirm your name, please?" he asked, after a quiet gasp at his end.

"Cai Chun-Bin," she said simply, eyes watching her perimeter, even as Chace was set to draw and fire if anyone got too close.

"Stand by, Miss Cai," he said. "I will transfer you now."

Hold music. K-Pop, but not a band she recognized. Pleasant enough.

"This is Manager Han," a gruffer voice came on the line. "How may I be of assistance, Miss Cai?"

"What is the status of the operation?" she asked simply.

"Holding pattern," he replied. "Ready to bring you in. What do you need?"

"Pickup," she told him, marveling at how Chace had been able to say a single word to get everything he needed into motion.

She needed to plan and reorganize things better, after this.

"Where are you?" Guanting asked.

She gave him an intersection several blocks east, closer to downtown, just as Chace had done last night. Only last night? Less than eighteen hours ago?

"Be there in ten minutes," she ordered.

"We will be," he replied. "Call on this number?"

"Yes."

She hung up and Chace nodded. She fell in beside him, close but not holding hands in case someone had been monitoring that line. Some mole in her organization like Chace had found in his.

They walked. The crowds were thinning a bit as the heat ramped up. Nasty hot coming, but not quite yet. Get off the streets until dark, then come out to prey on a few folks?

She liked that idea.

Rowena looked up at Chace, noting his concern.

"You'll be safe," she said. "Or I will put you on an airplane myself and get you out of country."

"Need to stop by my hotel and grab a few things before we do that," he grinned. "Passport and stuff are in the safe."

She nodded, wondering how many passports he really had. And under how many different names.

Part of her was concerned that she might be inviting a tiger into her home, but there was so much she needed to know about this man, over and above her father's questions.

Who was Chace Haig? And did she need to kill him to keep her father safe? It had been a lifetime ago. Could they negotiate a treaty that let everyone be, at least long enough to go after the assassins? Longer?

They walked. The streets weren't full, but busier than they had been last night. Her phone rang.

She answered it left-handed, ready to draw and shoot, even as Chace did the same.

"Where are you?" she asked.

"Standing next to a black Mercedes sedan," the man answered. "Southwest corner."

Rowena looked and saw the man across the intersection.

"I will be there in ninety seconds," she said. "Stay on the line and talk as if to a friend while I ignore you."

"Understood," he said, then began a rambling story about a baseball game he'd been to recently.

She tuned it out, watching the crowd as they crossed the street and got closer.

"I am on your right," she said, watching him perk up and turn, nodding as he cut the line and opened the rear door for her in a single motion.

Chace motioned for her to enter first, still watching.

Rowena slid in, waiting for Chace to follow.

TWENTY-EIGHT

Chace had rated her organization against the sort of scale he maintained in his head. Not all that bad, either, considering that he was pretty certain it was entirely civilian. Likely advised by retired spooks, and China had been stable long enough to have true professionals available.

The car wasn't all that heavily armored, from the way it rode. Possibly good enough. The man looked too much like a thug and not a chauffeur.

Still, adequate.

And if he got into that car, though, he was committed. Up until this moment, he could have bolted at any time, had he needed. Turned a corner at a dead run and never looked back. Something.

But nothing had jumped out and spooked him, so he was with her.

And now?

He drew a breath and focused on his cover. On how a dangerous Swiss banker used to dealing with criminal misfits would handle this situation. Up until now, he'd been stone pro, going back to that agent he'd been before becoming Chace Haig.

Chace let some of that go and nodded to the guy with the door, slipping in and letting the man close them up.

Committed.

The car slipped into traffic. Rowena reached over and took his hand, so he held hers, even as he memorized the route they took and watched for motorcycles suddenly driving up next to them with an armed passenger.

Nasty assassination trick, if your target's car wasn't armored. The doors on the Mercedes hadn't slammed hard enough. Maybe kevlar inside them, but nothing heavier.

Near as he could tell, they were headed south. Office buildings and warehouses began to mix. The two men up front didn't speak, watching the streets as well. Rowena held his hand. Chace watched the city roll by.

After fifteen minutes, they turned into an open garage door that closed behind them quickly. The car came to rest and shut off. The two up front looked back for instructions.

"You wait here," Rowena ordered, opening her door.

Chace joined her outside, looking around. A few shipping containers close by. Tall racks and shelves beyond that, with both an overhead crane and forklifts in constant motion. Workers, moving things around but largely ignoring them.

Hopefully ignoring them. Easy way to slip someone in, if her people had minimum wage people pulling things out of containers and putting them up for access. The biggest book company in the world had transformed itself into a logistics operation that way, providing a marketplace for anything and constantly building new warehouses everywhere to make it faster to deliver goods to people.

This wasn't one of those, but it had much the same flavor as Rowena quickly crossed to a closed door and went through.

Into an elevator and up, though she didn't push any buttons. Someone watching on a camera, Chace assumed.

At the top, the doors slid open and he followed her into a small operations control room. Consoles with security camera displays. Men with headsets watching and occasionally typing. Lights dim but not dark. Not a lot of conversation.

How many places were they watching from here? Smugglers would need to take care, in case the authorities suddenly showed up in a raid.

Assuming you hadn't corrupted the right people ahead of time. Chace was something of an expert on knowing the right people to do that.

All this felt too open, but he followed her through into another space. Conference room this time. Tall Chinese man standing. Two more off to one side, looking like gophers more than decision makers.

"Han Jing-Li, this is Chace Haig," Rowena introduced the man. "Chace, Jing-Li is in charge of operations for Tokyo, when we need to do something."

Chace nodded. He doubted that she meant office manager. Not Thane's equivalent, because that person would be in Hong Kong. And might be Rowena herself, but he didn't ask. Didn't press.

They shook hands, got settled. A carafe of coffee got delivered and poured.

Han watched him with nervous eyes. Chace pretended not to notice.

"What have we missed?" Han asked Rowena.

Chace listened to Rowena give a pretty solid rundown of things, starting with a guy apparently named Dragon Scholar Zheng stepping out of the crowd and getting himself a concussion, all the way down to the two of them sitting at this table. Han had injected questions and observations as they went, but mostly listened.

Chace mentally upgraded his already-high opinion of Rowena Cai another notch as she spoke.

Han was still askance when he looked at Chace.

"He's on our side for now," Rowena instructed the man. And she was giving Han orders, from the way he nodded. Not satisfied, but unwilling to challenge her. "We have the same enemies and the same desire to see payback for being chased all over Tokyo. Have you notified my father?"

"We have," Han nodded deeply. "He was awaiting your debrief before speaking with you, in case we needed to move suddenly."

"Make sure you upgrade your security another notch for the next few days," Rowena said. "They may make another attempt."

Chace approved. He had no idea who those people really were, but they might get pissy, if they thought that their target was on the verge of escaping them. He'd seen it with criminal gangs, and undercover espionage really only differed in degree and budget, not context or personality.

Rowena smiled over at him now.

"Last night, you got to spend two hours on the phone explaining things," she said. "Jing-Li will get you settled and you can have a shower and a nap while I take my turn on the firing line. After that, perhaps an early dinner and we can start our hunt?"

"Looking forward to it," Chace said, noting that nobody had asked him anything to this point. Merely accepted Rowena's story as gospel and moved on.

If so, he had a pretty good legend going. It would be rude to blow up a Taiwanese intelligence operational cell in Tokyo, but it did fit with his cover.

And they'd started it.

Chace Haig was a criminal, not a spy. Didn't mean you got to muss his hair without repercussions. And Thane had given him a green light, because it might get him into a similar office in Hong Kong.

Hopefully, one he could escape from later, if the man across the table ended up being Cai Yan-Li instead of some mid-level manager.

"Let us get you settled," Han said, rising. "We have clothes that should fit, given your narrow build."

Chace smiled. Anything purchased from China or Japan tended to be Asian sizes, which were a lot smaller than what you got in an American store. This was one time when long and lean would be to his benefit.

He nodded to Rowena and followed Han deeper into this complex that seemed to fill the space above the warehouse floor. Through a double door, it got positively cozy, with deep maroon carpets, various art on the walls and plants strewn about. Down a couple of side corridors, Han pulled out a keycard and opened the locks on a door, then handed it to Chace.

"Let me know if you have any questions," Han said politely. "Suite for visitors. Mistress Cai will be just down the hall, once she gets done, at least until she determines her plans. Will it be acceptable to send a tailor in two hours?"

"It will," Chace agreed.

"Excellent, sir," Han said, stepping back and withdrawing.

Chace entered and found himself in a place similar to the safe house.

Or the hotel he'd left yesterday. Only so many ways to do something like this, and he lived in hotel rooms all over the world.

Quickly, he scouted everything. Front room with wet bar. Bathroom with full shower instead of sitting. Plus a soaking tub, for extra decadence. King sized bed with entertainment system at the foot.

All of the heaviness of the last eighteen hours seemed to weigh heavily on him now. Chace went old-fashioned and propped a chair under the door handle, then went to take a shower.

Rowena waited until she was alone, then picked up the handset on the phone.

"What do you think?" she asked.

"I think we can use him," Father replied. "Should we use him up in the process?"

Rowena considered a number of responses. Father had been briefed and had been listening in silently on the conversation, but hadn't seen Chace move. Or think. Or call on resources far beyond what she had outside of China.

And he had been on vacation, half a world away from his home?

"I'm not entirely sure we could," she answered honestly. "He's good. Exceptional. And has made plain to me his disdain for our enemies and his interest in paybacks. I think we should use him to destroy as much of their operation as we can. After that, I am less certain."

"As am I, daughter," Father said. "It is good that you made it back safe, and I grow concerned that Haig is some sort of American spy, in spite of what you have seen and those few things we have learned here, once we started digging."

"Was the other man an American spy?" she asked.

"What are you suggesting, Second Daughter?" Father asked.

"This Chace was not, as near as I can tell, intended to be bait to draw you out," Rowena replied. "Everything suggests that we drew the KMT agents down on ourselves when we engaged him, but they didn't know who he was. Did they panic that we were about to expand our activities to Europe, after remaining quietly in Asia for so long?"

Father didn't reply, so she knew she'd hit on a solid point.

"Would an American spy allow that?" he finally asked, voice less hostile and more contemplative.

"Is he a spy for them?" she countered. "Or is he merely some sort of patriot, working for their interests while simultaneously trying to get rich? After all, doesn't that describe us? The Party is in charge today, and open to the West. At the same time, that was because we failed to to stop Deng when we had the chance. If we could close China down and drive out everyone, we would finally be successful. China for the Chinese, rather than the Manchu. Or the Han. Or the Tibetans. Or the rest of the colonial bastards that have bedeviled us for so long."

"Do you think you could cultivate him?" Father asked.

"He described himself as a man who finds other criminals for you, for a price," Rowena said. "What if we asked—if I asked—him to introduce us to someone in Egypt or Britain or somewhere that could facilitate more shipping? More smuggling? China and Russia will never be friends. Siberia is lying there prostrate as the Russian Empire continues to implode. India blocks us to the southwest. But Egypt opens us up to the Middle East and the Med. Britain used to get us Europe, but now we need Holland or Germany. And then there is the United States. Could Haig open us up a new frontier that lets China fully colonize them instead? Already, Japanese and Korean cars are manufactured there. China is rising, but the Americans will move to thwart us, as they did the Japanese forty years ago. Should we ask Chace to get us a foot in the door there ahead of time?"

More silence. She'd given this a lot of thought, because if he was really a spy for the CIA or someone, he would balk at some point. Pull back, and she'd know the truth.

If he wasn't—if he really was merely an exceptionally dangerous banker—if he could be *merely* anything—then that opened up a new frontier.

China could do unto the West, having been too weak for so long that they could not resist the colonial powers.

"You will walk a dangerous path, daughter," Father told her after a long pause. "I am not certain that you will succeed, but I agree that the opportunities presented, however accidental they might be, would let us extend our reach and power. Possibly expose more of our enemies, that we can crush them. Chairman Xi will not rest until Taiwan returns to the fold, but I am not certain that anything short of total war could manage such a thing, and the Americans will resist. Worse, if a war comes, Hong Kong will suffer greatly."

"Where will we move to?" she asked, knowing that Father was pursuing a plan he had inherited from five generations of ancestors.

One he expected her to pursue in turn.

Power. Money, to a lesser degree, because money could move people, but you needed raw power at the end of the day.

"Plans are already in motion," Father told her. "When you return, we will go deeper into things, but first you must solve the question of Chase Haig."

"I intend to, Father," Rowena replied. "I intend to."

Thane had to call certain analysts into her office for updates, in spite of her preference to go see them, because more than half of the building didn't need to know anything substantive about Chace. Even at the level of security clearance needed first, if you even got to know know this building existed.

Emily Rolland. Young woman. Mousy but smart. Newly minted PhD in PolSci with an emphasis on Sino-Japanese studies. Exactly the sort of person Thane needed for background. And answers.

The door was closed.

"How will the Japanese respond, given that?" Thane asked, having heard the woman's background briefing on the broader situation.

"They know they are a playground for spies," the woman nodded. "Much like Berlin was in the old days. Or London more recently. Koreans. Taiwanese. Chinese. Russians. Mostly industrial espionage, rather than more overtly political, but that's the Soviet Union collapsing, China opening up, and Asia turning into an industrial powerhouse. In this case, they're likely to be pissed at the Taiwanese government, but willing to cut some slack because China is on another rant. Taiwan's Vice President is transiting the US on the way to South America. That's always good for extra aircraft incursions and missile tests. Japan is planning to ramp up military expenditures yet again, with more warships and aircraft, because they expect China to launch an invasion sooner rather than later."

"Why is that?" Thane asked, looking for places where Chace or another operative might need to be inserted.

"Ukraine showed how hard it is to conquer a modern country equipped with sophisticated arms," Rolland said. "Granted, the Russian army had been hollowed out for at least a generation if not longer, but everyone expected more. Taiwan is also separated by a hundred miles of ocean, so China would have to add an amphibious landing fleet on top of that. Since the US is in the process of delivering billions of dollars of Harpoon missiles on top of the other things we've sold or delivered, that really puts a deadline on when a Chinese fleet could launch a naval assault and not expect to be immediately sunk. Throw in the US, Australia, and Japan backstopping, and it gets ugly."

"Will China let Taiwan go?" Thane asked.

"No, and they are more likely to go scorched earth if they can't win," Rolland nodded. "Think Odessa or Kyev, but with competent commanders launching a lot more missiles. Maybe small nuclear weapons as well, because they might be willing to end Taiwan entirely. Burn them rather than let them escape."

Thane leaned back and grimaced.

"You will not repeat this," Thane instructed the woman. "Ever. I have an agent in Tokyo right now. He is attempting to penetrate a Chinese criminal organization with deep ties to the Party on a variety of levels. That's what drew these KMT dipshits out of the woodwork. I want you to find out who these Taiwanese really are and where to find them, in case I need to leak things to the Japanese government. Questions?"

"How big a splash do you need to be prepared to make?" Rolland asked.

"Field agents and their immediate supervisors," Thane said. "I want to know everything we have on Dragon Scholar Zheng and his boss."

"Johnathon Kwok," Dr. Rolland replied instantly. "*Manager* Kwok. If they were organized like us, he'd be the man running agents in the field and reporting directly to you. We don't have a lot on him at present, because he's kept a remarkably low profile to date."

"Dig," Thane replied. "My agent might need to go after the man as part of his cover, and I'd like him to win in the process. File it with me directly, and let me know day or night, because he's operating thirteen hours off us."

"Understood, ma'am," Rolland said. "Anything else?"

"Go," Thane replied.

Once she was alone, she sighed and considered just how much she might need to adjust Haig's operations over the next few years.

If he survived all this.

She also wondered if she was about to start a small war with Taiwan herself.

And who else she'd piss off in the process.

Chace had put on a nice robe after showering. Turned on a bit of news just to see if anything useful had come up, but most of it was in Chinese or Japanese, and he didn't feel like trying to follow, so he'd ended up finding a channel playing some old jazz. Soothing. The sort of thing that had come with the name, because the original man had been a jazz aficionado, back in the day.

It had grown on him.

A knock and Chace moved to open the door, meeting a tiny Japanese man with serious eyes, escorted by Han.

He spoke sharply, but Chace hardly understood.

"He asked you to dress in your previous clothing, so that he can see how it wears," Han translated.

Chace did, quickly getting back to where he'd been. The tailor walked around him twice, muttering, then pulled a tape measure and quickly got Chace's specifics.

"One hour," he announced in broken English. "Strip and I wash."

Chace did, back into his robe, and was alone again, wondering what he would be wearing this afternoon. Laundry would be nice, but the man had the promise of a new suit—or something—in his eyes.

He settled for music and a glass of orange juice from the bar's refrigerator. Another knock fifteen minutes later turned out to be Rowena, hair a little damp and in new clothes.

Chace moved to the chair and she settled on the sofa across from him, eyes glittering.

"How do you feel about playing a violent practical joke on someone?" she asked.

"We tracking down the guy I put in the hospital?" he asked.

"Partly," she replied. "He was treated and released. The one you shot is supposedly scheduled to fly to Taiwan tomorrow on a special aircraft."

"What are you planning?" he asked.

From the moment he'd gotten into that Mercedes, he's surrendered some freedom of motion. Some agency. She needed to be comfortable enough to bring him in and protect him from her own people, who were obviously too keyed up about his name.

As long as nobody offered to haul him to Hong Kong as part of this, he should be fine. Chace had no doubt that her father would greet whatever plane landed, surrounded by heavily armed goons and wanting to ask some pointed questions.

"We've been asking the underworld for tips," Rowena said, grinning harshly. "Offering outsized bribes for tidbits, partly to see who we might turn or blackmail later, and if we could roust those KMT punks into trying something stupid."

"Gotten anywhere?" Chace perked up.

Part of his job involved surfacing criminals to the point that other agencies, espionage or law enforcement, could track them down later. Or eliminate them.

Did Rowena understand that she might be risking that? Possibly not, from her smile.

"We have some bits," she nodded sagely. "A tea house where they occasionally linger. A warehouse that might hold more than it seems. An office that might be a front for what my people would consider a terrorist cell, though the locals and your people probably don't agree."

"My people have apologized for hanging my ass out to dry twice," he reminded her. "They won't complain too much if I take matters into my own hands on this."

Her eyes got a little big as she absorbed that.

Technically, what he was proposing might be treason. Or at least giving aid and comfort to the enemy, but he was Chace Haig, and the International Legal Research Institute had been created specifically because the US Government sometimes needed an operative so deep cover that they couldn't even *tell themselves* about it. A blunt or sharp instrument that they could entirely deny, if pressed.

He did things that would get him hung in many countries, if someone didn't slip in and blow his cover so that someone had to get him out.

None of them had ever been caught at it, but he woke up every morning knowing that he was playing the odds.

At the same time, he might be pulled deeper into her organization, one that Thane might not have known existed, because it had supposedly been smashed by Chace Haig in 1988.

Tightrope time.

"Would you be okay assisting us in raiding the office?" she asked carefully.

"You want prisoners, martyrs, or victims?" he asked in an ugly ugly tone.

How messy did you want to get, if dealing with some sort of deep-cover KMT assassination squad still fighting the Civil war seventy-five years later?

"We want information," she countered. "Break in and steal a bunch of computers that we can turn over to some on-staff hackers to crack open."

"Air-gapped systems?" he asked.

Chace knew far more about computers than any of his predecessors, but that was the world moving on from what it had been in 1962.

Most computers were connected to the internet somehow. Able to be accessed from anywhere in the world, if you had the right credentials. The North Koreans and Russians had built entire industries around hacking into various corporate and governmental systems, either for juvenile delinquency, sabotage, or stealing things. Wannabe Cryptobros were morons when it came to electronic security, so their wallets were constantly being drained of billions.

The safest way to protect a computer was to not connect it to any network outside. Literally keep all the machines on an internal-only network. Really hard to break in and steal your data, without literally breaking in first. *Air-gapped.*

"We assume so," Rowena agreed. "Very few hints that these people even existed before this, and we would have encountered them before, so either they were brought to Tokyo because I was coming, or they were already here and got activated. Either way, it's a means by which we can damage them."

"You want the building burned down afterwards?" he asked, mostly to see how far she would go.

Chace had no doubts that she was looking for the line past which he wouldn't go. Every agent had one, based on the limits of their mission or orders.

Chace was one of an extremely few free agents. Intentionally.

Specifically for this reason.

"I don't think we'll need to go that far," she said quietly. "But I reserve the right to change my mind later. You don't care?"

"I plan on going back to America or Europe when I'm done here," he nodded. "And asking for a few favors from folks there, in case Taiwanese Intelligence gets up on their high horse. The Russians hate those folks almost as much as they hate the Japanese or Chinese, so they'd be happy to interfere with folks trying to get to me. If I have to burn a few bridges in Tokyo, it wasn't like I was planning on coming back here anytime soon. Or Taipei."

She flinched. Wasn't much, but he was watching for exactly that reaction from the woman. Not ready to take this to the logical conclusion, because that might turn into a full-scale war in the shadows. Those places where darkness obscured everything, and you had to rely on the night sounds for any warning that trouble was coming.

He smiled. It was not a pleasant smile, but he relaxed it.

"Maybe we can do something and draw them all out?" he pivoted now. "Get the place emptied out of people and we can slip in and out before they can respond?"

"How would you do it?" she asked, intrigued.

"Plant a fake leak," he nodded. "Time and place somewhat remote, where one of their people expects us to be. Kind of like a dinner reservation, but the sort of people and place you'd go if you were hiring a mercenary hit team yourself. Assuming you don't have those people on staff already."

"I have a few," she nodded coyly. "But I like the idea of leaking a recruiting meeting."

"Better, reach out and set up such a meeting," he offered. "Don't actually go, obviously, but offer to pay the folks up front for an evening of them listening to your proposals, so they aren't pissed at you later. Help that to leak a little, then maybe our friends will be there, waiting for you to arrive."

"I like it," she nodded. "Subtle, but effective. How good are you at the breaking and entering side of things?"

Chace shrugged, wondering how much she should know.

"I'm exceptional at social engineering," he replied. "And stealth. Reasonable at physical security, but computers themselves aren't usually my thing. I hire experts when I need a laptop or something, calling in favors from those sorts of people. That help?"

"It does," she nodded. "I'm a computer programmer in my spare time. Mostly databases and InfoSec—Information Security—so I know the electronics bits."

"Sounds like one hell of a team," Chace smiled. "Throw in a driver and a spotter that stay with the car?"

"Yes," she nodded, rising and moving close enough to kiss him once before withdrawing. "I'll start getting things in motion."

And he as alone.

At least until he got back into the field.

And they'd started it.

Rowena called Han into the office she was using. This was more like their normal relationship, because he worked for her at the end of the day. And was nervously aware of the shortcomings that the last two days had revealed in his intelligence gathering.

And operational security.

"This is your chance to redeem yourself, Jing-Li," she told him as he settled, enjoying that jolt of fear that she saw in his eyes.

His wasn't a job where you retired someplace. He knew too much, so if he was no longer useful in Tokyo, it would time to return to Hong Kong and vanish into one of father's other companies.

Assuming that he didn't turn out to be so dangerous or incompetent that he needed to simply disappear permanently.

Redeem was the key here. He had fucked up, but not terminally. And she was willing to own some level of error here, because she'd gone at Chace Haig openly, thus revealing herself to folks nobody had anticipated.

The two sides hadn't gotten openly violent at each other in Tokyo in more than a decade.

Something had changed. She supposed that she owed Chace an apology and a thank you for breaking it all out into the open.

"Ma'am?" Han asked carefully.

"I want you to contact the Morishita Clan," she told him. "I want to meet with someone mid-level important at nine pm, at a location they specify in Arakawa, to talk about hiring some experts at violence. Pay them up front for their time, then let me know what the arrangements are. Are you clear so far?"

"So far, yes," he nodded. "We'd already contacted them about a possible retainer on your father's orders, so they will be prepared."

"Good," Rowena replied. "I will need a driver and a spotter, both armed and the best you have. A low-profile sedan. Chace and I will access the storage closet for certain gear we need before we head out."

Something troubled him.

"Yes?" Rowena asked.

"We could just as easily bring Morishita here to talk," he said. "Safer, too, and they are not likely to object."

"Understood," Rowena nodded. "I want you to leak the details of the meeting to a few folks we suspect of being paid under the table for such information. And keep track of who knew, but do not act on it now. I'll interview them myself later."

"Ah, because you won't be there," he nodded, much more confident. "Wild goose chase. Where will you be?"

"You don't need to know," Rowena informed the man. "That way, nobody will know ahead of time and can't stop us. Be prepared to abandon this facility on short notice if something goes wrong. In fact, once Chace and I are equipped, start removing all critical systems and personnel to safe houses for at least two days. I have reviewed your notes and will assign the flat in Edogawa to myself and Chace, so keep your other people west of the river. Questions?"

Han shook his head.

"Operational things, so nothing you need to be immediately concerned about," he replied. "I can route questions to Hong Kong or Kowloon for certain things. Thank you for this chance to redeem myself, mistress."

"You couldn't have seen this coming, Han," Rowena emphasized, reminding him that he wasn't entirely at fault. "I didn't, and should have. We'll make the best of it, but things might get messy for a time."

"Open warfare in the streets again?" he asked, perking up.

Han had been a young soldier in the messiness that had come and gone around the time the Soviet Union imploded and Russia had turned into a free-for-all as privatization took hold. Vladivostok was still a den of smuggling and crime that her Father and grandfather had taken advantage of.

Hopefully, she didn't need to deal with those gangsters on top of everything else right now, but she'd handle it. Or maybe ask Chace for some contacts to eliminate some of those problem children, if he had the right kinds of contacts with the Russians.

She smiled at the thought.

"Entirely possible," Rowena said simply. "I'm going to do a thing. The KMT will take exception, but might not be able to stop me. Or catch me later, as I will withdraw from Japan quickly once it is complete, hopefully drawing their eye and ire back to Canton with me."

"Understood," Han said, rising. "If that's all?"

"Go," she nodded, then fell back into herself when the door closed.

Chace could open all manner of new options, even if he was a patriot and spy, since few people liked the Russians right now. And nobody trusted them at all.

How far could that carry her?

When would Chace balk? Or would he? Had someone been doing this for forty years under that name?

The implications of such a program left Rowena utterly cold. That was beginning to approach Chinese levels of patience, which was one of her people's great hidden strengths.

The family had been working at this for almost two hundred years. Americans weren't supposed to understand that sort of commitment.

Worse, there was no way to determine the truth about the man without pushing too far. Or asking him to his face.

How badly did she need to know the truth?

Chace was impressed. That tiny tailor had returned with a stylish new suit expertly perfect in fit, plus his old suit, plus an outfit he could only classify as battle gear.

Medium gray, instead of black, because the night is hardly ever that dark. Lace up boots with sides that breathed. Baggy pants with American BDU style cargo pockets. Baggy pullover shirt. Even a silk scarf he could wrap like a shemagh to hide from cameras. Or break up his silhouette.

He felt like a ninja in it. Looked like one, too.

Rowena wolf-whistled at him, so he turned away from the mirror and smiled at her.

"Keeping the SIGs?" he asked, skipping over all the banter and getting serious.

"And have gotten an extra magazine for each in the gear pouches we'll have with us," she nodded. "Jacketed softnose rounds, like you had before, so they should fire the same if you have to."

"How big is the team?" he asked.

"The two of us," she turned serious. "Misdirection should have most of our foes up north and out of the way. Driver and spotter in the car, with encrypted tactical headsets. We'll get in and out as quickly as we can, stealing anything that looks worth taking. Then a safe house because we're evacuating this facility for a few days, just in case."

"Wise move," he agreed. "The folks left out in the cold might unleash a spasm of violence in response. How soon until we leave?"

Mid-afternoon, after he'd been going like hell for nearly thirty hours, broken only by time to meditate this morning and this afternoon. He hadn't actually slept at any point, but knew he could push himself another twelve or eighteen hours before he started making bad decisions because he was too fatigued.

"Dinner will be ready in a bit," she said. "Sun will set in three hours, and our misdirection meeting is an hour after that. Do you need to sleep?"

"I'll eat and crash a little," he decided. "Mostly meditation, like before. I can sleep when we're done."

Something she wanted to ask him, but she held it back. He could see that in her eyes. In her stance.

It would come out eventually. Or not. They were all adults around here.

And Chace was already on thin-enough ice without additional issues.

"Coffee or tea?" she asked.

"Coffee," he decided. "I'll crash later, but need to be sharp now."

"Let's get you settled then," Rowena said, taking his hand and drawing him back out of the suite and into the rest of the building.

They went a different direction he hadn't seen earlier, and ended up in something his mind wanted to call an executive lunchroom. Nicer than the guards would get. Sushi chef standing ready for maki, sashimi, or sushi, as needed.

It was always nice, working with a client who kept a personal chef on staff. And he had to treat her like another client, at least until he understood what her limits were. Where she saw him fitting into the picture.

Young woman, but exceptionally sharp and mature for twenty-seven. He could only imagine how much better she was likely to get with another decade of experience. Up in Thane's league at that point, possibly.

How long term could he stretch this mission, if Rowena Cai was interested in more than his contacts?

Chace smiled and ordered as the waitress came to their table.

"What?" Rowena asked when they were alone again.

"You are trouble," he said with a grin. "Wondering how much."

"Afraid you can't keep up?" she teased.

"I'm not twenty-one anymore," he admitted with mock-severity. "Gotta pace myself with a dangerous woman."

She grinned.

"How much trouble did you want?" she asked in a tone that could be interpreted as serious or silly as you wanted.

"I'm never looking for trouble," Chace admitted. "It sneaks up on me occasionally. Like you. Trying to figure out what overmorrow looks like."

"Overmorrow?" Her eyes crossed in the cutest way.

"Old English term for the day after tomorrow," he told her. "Tomorrow, chickens in hen houses as things get sorted out. Depending on how much damage we do tonight, I might have to lay low for a week. Or find someone to smuggle me out someplace where I can fly to a safe destination."

"Hong Kong not safe?" she asked, possibly hurt. Possibly setting a trap.

"Don't know the town," Chace acknowledged. "Or the people. Your home turf, and I don't even know if there's some guy back there who might take exception to me being around you."

The way he phrased it suggested a boyfriend, but also left open her father, whatever Yan-Li Cai thought. Or how angry the man might be for the sins of the fathers.

"I don't have a boyfriend to get jealous," she said, possibly leaving off her father as well. "Worse come to worst, we can get you to Hong Kong. Or possibly Seoul, if we want folks looking the wrong direction for you. For us."

Us? That suggested a few days together on a boat. Yachts were nice. Cargo vessels tended to be old and grimy, regardless of the romance of such things in books.

"We'll just have to play it by ear, then," he offered as a marker.

The first maki arrived at that moment, so they concentrated on food.

Overmorrow would already be here too soon.

Rowena watched Chace organize himself in the equipment closet. Without knowing where anything was, he asked the armorer specific, deliberate questions, acquiring a compact set of gear that looked like something she should just go ahead and have permanently arranged in some sort of travel kit after this.

Lockpicks and a snap gun, the latter designed to be inserted into a lock, activated, then twisted hard enough to jolt any common lock into opening, often without leaving marks that someone had picked it or damaging the frame. Pocket flashlight with a clip and a bendable neck, so he could usse it without needing a hand. Zip ties for holding things, including people. Small digital camera made from a cell phone with no sim card and a lot of data space inside.

Rowena was mostly surprised when he went for an American flash-bang grenade. Loud and stunning in a confined space, but almost no shrapnel. His smile promised a level of expertise with the weapon she wasn't necessarily prepared for as she handed her earplugs that would deaden the sound without deafening her.

When he found the silencers, Chace immediately discarded the SIG he had and found one already threaded to accept such a device, having her do the same thing as the armorer supervised.

All of this spoke to a man highly trained in violent entry to hostile premises. Rowena found herself learning odd tidbits that Chace took for granted.

Rowena had a small computer system she'd previously built for this sort of thing. A Raspberry Pi device she'd upgraded, along with a keyboard she could attach, a battery pack good for a few hours of use, and a small tablet computer monitor with the wifi card physically removed to prevent it inadvertently giving her away.

With what she had loaded on the Pi, Rowena was confident that she could access any system, because she could plug into some computer, even powered down, and mount the local drives as if externals, then rapidly pull down whole folder trees for later use.

Assuming she didn't just grab a laptop and dump it into her messenger bag for later. Or steal a NAS device—Network-Attached Storage, which was just a fancy term for a block of hard drives anyone could access remotely. Those tended to be common, small, and encrypted if people were paying attention.

Rowena was willing to bet she had the tools to crack any encryption scheme eventually. Or the contacts. Or maybe she'd ask Chace for help finding some underemployed Russian hackers she could add to her list.

It was good.

A quick bio break and they were in motion, this time riding in a blacked out SUV. Not one of the monsters that had a hard time navigating Tokyo's narrower streets, but big enough for four comfortably and dark enough to look tough.

Chace had grimaced when he saw the vehicle.

"Problems?" she'd asked.

"Too high profile," he muttered. "Stands out. You want an old beater. Gray and faded. Dirty. Smoky windows without complete darkness. This looks like something a spy or crime lord drives around in, when he wants to intimidate people."

"Interesting," she'd nodded. "I shall have to engage your design sensibilities later."

"I work cheap," he grinned.

Now they were almost to their destination. And Rowena had noted how invisible other vehicles tended to be, when she could suddenly see this beast standing out.

But if he was that long-term an operation, she could see his expertise had been hiding in plain sight. And needed to borrow some of that. Especially if they were about to start another round of open warfare with the Manchu escapees.

"Circle twice," Chace had ordered the driver. "Once close, then the second time on a larger circle where we'll drop. You'll stay at a distance where you can be to the front or rear door in thirty seconds from a call, even if you have to run a light."

The man had glanced at her, and gotten her nod, before accepting Chace's order. It was a good one. Different than she would have done it, but it was educational, watching a professional spy operate.

Chace might claim to be just a Swiss banker, but she'd long moved past that in her own head. And there was much she could learn from this man, in spite of previously thinking herself among the best. Perhaps the best of the amateurs? Food for thought.

The destination was an office building, old and worn, dirty and unappealing, but still lit up because it wasn't even nine o'clock. Most staff would head out to start drinking heavily soon, before staggering to the train station and possibly collapsing into a pod instead of taking the extra hour each way getting home.

The timing meant that they could get into the building before it had gone dark. Before cleaners would come to prepare it for tomorrow. When accountants and salarymen were getting tired and bleary, heads down all day and working themselves up to a night of drinking with the boss and coworkers, because *Japan, Inc.* didn't believe in any sort of home life.

The government wondered why there were fewer children every generation. And why husbands who finally retired often found themselves divorced quickly by wives that had turned into complete strangers.

Rowena shook her head and kept watch. First ring solid. Nobody obviously watching the space, but they wouldn't be. It would be cameras somewhere with a view, and a question of how sharp the watchers were.

The second ring was a wider net.

"Turn right into that alley just ahead," Chace suddenly barked.

"Stop long enough for us to get out, then complete this loop and a second one before coming to rest."

Sudden, unexpected, still in pattern. Rowena liked it, and wondered what lessons there were as the vehicle slid to a halt in a dark spot and they both jumped out.

"One, two," Chace said into the microphone.

"Confirmed," the passenger replied instantly.

Rowena turned to confirm that nobody was following them. Chace joined her a second later.

"You ready?" he asked.

Chace had added a light jacket to the outfit. It covered up things and let him blend better into the suit-coated businessmen making their way around Tokyo, in spite of his height.

Rowena had a similar look, though pants were less common than dresses on women. She nodded and fell in beside him as they doubled back. Nobody appeared to be following the truck, which was good. And why he'd chosen this alley. Dark and wide, but isolated.

Someone would have had to break pattern and driven in here, coming right at them. Chace would see how well armored their windshield was at that point.

Silenced or not, a 9mm round at short range had a lot of punch. And he'd gone ahead and screwed the tube on, though he'd left it in the holster for now. Slower and harder to draw, but no louder than a sneeze when he'd loaded subsonic ammunition for it.

They'd started it.

Out on the sidewalk, they fell into the evening crowd of pedestrians. Less tourists in this area, but the folks around them had already worked a full day and now had a night of drinking with the boss to look forward to. He could see exhaustion in their eyes as they walked around him like well-dressed zombies in gray and black.

Better that way, as few of them would register or remember him and

Rowena later, especially with a mask around the bottom half of his face, like everyone else.

Chace wondered how much fun he might cause if he added eyes and features to a mask design intended to cause AI camera systems to read false negatives when trying to make a face match. There were hyperso-phisticated systems out there, doing the pattern-matching, but every extra variable he could add would make things that much harder.

They crossed two blocks carefully, moving with the flow of folks. Chace walked a bit hunched, so he was less obvious. Hiding in plain sight.

They got to the alley he wanted and turned in without breaking stride. Normal folks out for normal business. Nothing to draw the eye, officer.

There was a loading dock and a smaller lobby back here that connected around to the front, but didn't have a guard sitting at the desk. After hours, so the man up front was alone, watching on a camera, no doubt.

Chace went in first, Rowena close on his heels, then crossed to the elevator bank and pressed the up button. He concentrated on projecting an image of someone who had forgotten something upstairs and needed to grab it before heading out on a date, Rowena holding his hand now and touching arms as she stood close.

This was the critical moment. Would any of the assassins have seen them enter the building and rushed to the elevator? Was he about to be in a fight or gun battle, right here in the lobby?

How solid was their misdirection this evening, hopefully having drawn the Dragon Scholar north and west?

The next elevator arrived and opened, spilling out a mob of folks. Chace concentrated on faces, but most of the salarymen never looked up. Merely avoided him like a stone in a river, intent on whatever dreams and nightmares plagued those folks as they got close to the dark-ness outside.

Chace breathed a small sigh of relief and they entered the empty elevator.

He pushed the second button above their floor and they rode in silence, eventually arriving where an insurance company had a branch office for processing, according to his research. Hallway well lit. Doors showing light behind frosted glass that they ignored as they walked to a stairwell and went right in.

Always look like you know where you are going. Furtive people set off alarms in even the most casual watchers, and this building held dangerous secrets. Deadly people.

Down two flights, Chace rested. He turned to Rowena and nodded.

"Go ahead and draw now," he instructed her. "Walk with it down against your thigh. Only shoot if they are too far away for me to punch them, okay?"

"Understood," she nodded.

Chace went ahead and pulled out his snap gun, also holding it like a pistol, low at his side as he opened and stepped into the hallway.

Down and around a corner. The door he wanted was on the left. Chace walked right up and put the snap gun against the lock and slid it in, then gave it a snap and a twist. The tool forced all the pins up, just like a normal key would, without the ridges to get them correctly. Instead, a sharp turn while they were up and Chace was able to turn the lock.

Another choke point. They had no way to know what the interior of the office might look like. Or who might be here.

And it wasn't like he could have called on some of his own folks to provide office blueprints stolen from somewhere. Not without telling Rowena more than she knew. Or maybe warning the Taiwanese that he was coming.

Assuming Rowena was somehow still ignorant of things and not stringing him along for some trap later.

Chace turned the lock in a smooth movement and stepped quickly into the room. There was a man behind the desk in a small reception area, headphones on and only slowly looking up from his cell phone at movement.

Chace charged.

Confusion gave way to surprise on his target's face. Then recognition. Then shock.

A hand lashed out to grab the desk phone. Or trigger an alarm. Something.

Chace swept that phone off the desk with one hand and punched the man as hard as he could with the other, leaning across the desk to reach.

The man's head snapped back. He probably would have flipped over backwards, but his knees hit the bottom of the desk inside and jarred it upwards, trapping him in place. The man's face flopped forward into a second punch, a hard cross this time aimed at the side of his head and neck.

Various martial arts talked about all sorts of vital strike points you could tap there to render a foe unconscious. Chace used a big fist to hit as many of them as he could, as hard as he could.

The man slid off the seat bonelessly as Chace raced around the desk, hanging up the phone just in case and confirming his target.

The room had been empty. Still was. Rowena had closed the front door and stood in a pistolero stance aimed at an inner door beside the desk. First person opening that door was likely a dead man, but they didn't have long.

If someone inside noticed the commotion, they would call for help on a phone, especially if they had their own camera view that let them see Rowena covering the door.

Chace zip-tied the man's hands behind him and left him be. A pistol and a keycard got liberated, then his wallet as well, all going into Rowena's messenger bag purse for now. If nothing else, Rowena's people ought to be able to blow the man's cover entirely and burn him as a spy.

Always the worst thing that could happen to someone in this business.

To be a shit, Chace unplugged the desk phone entirely and put it right back on the desk, where the prisoner would be hard pressed to even stand, let along reach.

The cell phone was still showing some porn video, with the headphone leaking tinny, cheesy music, so Chace ignored it. Anyone calling and it wouldn't ring beyond the headphones.

Still, useful. He killed the video and it went into the purse as well.

Never ignore the intelligence you can gain from someone's contact list. There was a reason he memorized phone numbers instead, and hardly ever answered his own phone, instead letting everything go to voicemail to be filtered by Thane's people later.

Good enough.

He rose, then drew his SIG, silenced and ready. At this point, he was probably shooting first unless he could get another good drop on someone with a fist.

Safety off, he drew a breath and studied the door.

Like getting into that car with Rowena this morning, he would be committing a whole next layer of trouble and messiness when he went through. At the same time, it would extend his legend to Asia, being an enemy of the KMT and the Taiwanese government. At least on paper.

More criminal types might reach out to see what he could do for them.

If he survived.

Chace reached for the door handle.

Rowena was on his flank as they went through into a darker space beyond. Lights at half, they came up on motion sensors as they detected Chace entering.

He went to the left as soon as he was in the space. Rowena slid right, letting the door close behind her and listening. Chace had talked about the night sounds. That ambient noise that conveyed things to the unconscious mind. Like impending trouble.

Nothing jumped out at her.

Bullpen with a dozen desks in clusters of four, done old school when monitors had been enormous, heavy boxes. A kitchen space on her right. Bathrooms on the left. Four offices across the back with doors closed and lights off.

Desks showed random papers, but no laptops immediately obvious that she should steal. Partly, that was a relief, because she didn't have time to crack the cases on several in order to extract the hard drives, and could only really carry one or two.

Quickly, they swept the bathrooms, Chace checking while she covered the room.

She nodded to the offices.

"Where do we start?" she asked.

Chace scowled thoughtfully, then walked the length of the space, looking at his feet.

"This one," he announced, trying the lock and nodding when it didn't turn.

She put her back to a sidewall and watched the rest of the room while he swapped for his snap gun, jammed it into the lock, and popped it open.

"Heh," he grunted quietly. "Gotcha, suckers."

He motioned her close, swapping places and weapons as she looked in.

And drooled a little bit.

Storage closet, from the looks various crap on shelves around the outside, but one whole corner was a small IT operation, a rack-mounted router below with a black cube about twenty-four centimeters on a side was above that. One blue light and four green ones, sitting on a shelf below a telephone punch box so old her father would have been able to wire it.

Rowena slipped deeper into the room and studied her prey. She recognized the device, but not the specific model number. And probably wouldn't be able to hack it directly anyway, except that she could put it into a lab and brute force the system.

"Good new, bad news," she said after a moment, glancing back at Chace by the door.

"Computers are not my strong suit," he admitted.

Rowena wondered if Chace understood how few men would be willing to admit to any shortcoming in front of a woman, especially one they were trying to impress.

"NAS," she told him. "Network-Attached Storage device. Basically, four big hard drives in an array. Probably RAID 5 but maybe something more sophisticated. Won't know until I get inside it and look around."

"Can you do that with the tools you brought?" he asked, eyes and gun still covering the main room.

"I could, but it will take too long," she admitted, willing to be possibly less than perfect with Chace.

It had become a matter of trust between them.

"Okay," he prompted.

"Easiest solution is unplugging it and walking out," she continued.

"Problem is it weighs about three kilograms, and has no carrying handle, so I have to hold it like a fishbowl. That will be obvious."

"Only until we get to the truck," he said. "Pretty sure they will realize they've been robbed pretty quickly, once someone comes to check on our buddy out front. Or gets back from your meeting, grumpy as hell because you never showed up. Alternatively, I can carry it under one arm like a stack of books. How sturdy it is?"

"Don't drop it, because it might be possible to open it up electronically later," Rowena nodded.

"Any of these yahoos dumb enough to write down a set of usernames and passwords because they are too lazy to remember them?" he asked cheekily.

Rowena started to say something tart, then caught herself.

They wouldn't, would they?

But then she remembered who she was dealing with. Spies tended to be extremely conservative in some parts of their operations, in spite of liking new technological toys. And Taiwanese culture, like China, venerated age over competence in many cases. Was there a senior manager around here who predated mass computers? She was too used to her own organization, where you pulled your weight or got out.

Rowena moved the device enough to look at the back. One network cable coming in, running a meter to the router below to it. One power cable.

She unplugged both and popped the power cable into her bag so she didn't have to dig anything up later.

The black box was an awkward weight. Too big to carry one handed. No carrying handle. Designed to sit atop a shelf and hold buckets and buckets of data.

She handed it to Chace and made her way to the other end of the offices, gun in hand, then stopped.

"How did you know that was the server room?" she asked, looking back.

His grin was knowing.

"Foot traffic on the carpet," he replied, nodding to the floor.

Looking down, Rowena saw the wear patterns. Heaviest at this end.

Lightest at that end. Like it was a door that was never opened, as opposed to folks coming in to brief the boss.

And the senior agent would be at this end. Closest to the bathroom. Farthest from the noise of the kitchen and server room fans.

Huh. Social engineering, indeed.

She tried the handle, found it unlocked, and followed her pistol into the room, just in case someone had been working quietly and not noticed the lights come up or noise. Chace had the brick in one hand and his own pistol, but he would be slowed down.

Nobody.

She looked under the desk, but the space was empty.

Expensively gorgeous. Better than she usually decorated her own offices, but she didn't go in for fancy paintings, plants or wood paneling. Not like this.

Book shelf on a sidewall held a random selection of stuff. Utterly random as she checked spines. Histories. Biographies. Murder mysteries. At least three romance science fiction books with werewolves on space-ships, when curiosity at the titles required her to pull them out and look at the covers.

Okay, then.

She moved back to the desk, sitting and studying it. Chace had mentioned social engineering. The middle drawer was locked, as were the three on the right. Old-fashioned calendar pad covered the desktop to protect it. Pen in a holder. Phone.

"Chace, I need these drawers open," she decided, moving to the door and trading places with the man.

THIRTY-SEVEN

Chace rested the black box on the desk as he moved around the back, rolling the chair into the corner out of his way. Middle drawer and a stack of bigger ones.

Given that they'd already caused a ruckus, he looked on the few papers on the desk and located a letter opener that got jammed into the middle drawer's gap and leveraged open.

Lock pin gave and he rolled it out. Some sort of notebook with Japanese characters, then Roman ones next to them. Stack of them, with most of them crossed out.

He slid it across the desk.

"This what you were looking for?" he asked.

Rowena moved closer and glanced, grabbing it into her bag with some of tonight's other treasures.

"Probably," she said. "Won't know until I get back. Are the three drawers worth opening?"

Chace stuck a hand into the messiness of the open middle drawer and rooted around. Breath mints, post-it notes, spare ball-point pens.

Ah, there we are.

He pulled out a small ring of keys, one of which was shorter than the rest. Slipping it into the top lock, it turned.

"How did you know?" she asked, watching both him and the door when he looked up.

"Social engineering," Chace acknowledged. "Boss probably not that savvy with technology. Keeps that notebook of what looked like old passwords locked in his drawer. I'm guessing he has that key on his ring, then uses this key to get to the rest. Lazy thinking, but I didn't see a space for a safe, without moving pictures around. Or tearing this place apart, and I feel like we've probably stolen something good with the brick."

She nodded, as if surprised at his logic, but Chace had to wonder how much his experience deep cover might put him in a fairly rare league. Was Asia not as prepared? Or did her organization not have to go toe-to-toe with the big players all that often?

Was he training her up to his standards?

Hell of a way to get invited deeper into her group. Assuming it wasn't a trap at some point where he opened a door and found her father standing there with a gun in his hand and a cold smile on his face.

Chace found a bottle of sake and two small glasses in the top drawer, along with a small pistol he considered stealing to trace. Except that he already knew who owned it, so it wasn't worth anything except as a trophy, and he didn't do trophies.

Middle drawer was spare paper and office supplies, none of which had any value when he rifled through them.

Bottom drawer held a laptop.

"Bingo," Chace announced, grabbing it and the power supply and standing up.

She smiled as he moved around and slipped it into her messenger bag. She leaned close and kissed him, though they didn't linger.

"We should leave immediately," she said. "I doubt that there is anything better we could steal here."

"Indeed," Chace agreed. "We've already stolen their peace of mind. The rest is just frosting."

They got to the front door and checked on the guy still woozy on the floor, but breathing fine and the concussion would wear off in a while. He might not even remember who had hit him, assuming no cameras recording things.

Probably were, but he had a mask on, same as Rowena. Not that it would be difficult to put two and two together after this.

Chace had the brick. Easier to carry two handed, as she'd said, thought he could make do with one if he had to.

"You're armed," he said. "I lead, and you can shoot around me if you have to, distracting them."

"Got it," she said, that messenger bag a lot heavier now than it had been.

Chace let her open the front door and stepped into the hallway. They would ride the elevators because he really didn't want to try twenty-three levels of stairs with the heavy hard drive he was carrying.

He pushed the call button with an elbow and they waited, her standing next to him like it was a date still. Like he'd gone into the office to grab the black device in his hands so he could take it home and work on it.

Something utterly innocent. You'll believe that, won't you?

Thirty seconds later, the door dinged and then opened.

Two security guards looked up at them in complete surprise.

CHAPTER
THIRTY-EIGHT

Rowena charged, catching the men off-guard, because they had the look of two men expecting to sneak up on her and Chace and capture them still robbing that office.

She wondered what alarm had been triggered, but didn't give it any more thought than that as she used the pistol in her hand to whip the man on the right.

He got a hand up and might have cracked some bones, but she didn't land the blow on the side of his head as she'd planned. Knocked him down. The silencer came off, maybe broken.

She kept moving forward, driving a shoulder into the second man and slamming both of them into the back of the elevator with a thud that jarred it like a small earthquake.

Both guards were armed with pistols, though she had the only one in hand. The second guard whooshed as she drove all the air out of his lungs, but he got a hand up and shoved her away.

Mass mattered, because she flew backwards, then bounced herself off the far side.

Rowena braced herself as the second guard attacked, throwing a fist at her. No, at her pistol hand. She blocked automatically, then got the stinger as he knocked the weapon out of her hand.

She kicked him in the knee to drive him back, then the elevator doors closed and the box began to descend. There was no time for anything, so she followed up on the first man, knocking his own pistol out of his hand as he drew and tried to do something.

Fighting was especially awkward in a space two meters deep by two and a half wide. And she was committed.

Follow-up blows and a second pistol hit the deck, even as the first guard began to recover. Rowena grabbed the second then threw him into his friend, both of them collapsing again. She went down with them, punching the nearest man in kidneys and neck and head and anything else she could reach, even as he tried to cover up, roll away, escape her.

A hand emerged and caught her wrist, so she threw punches at the other man. Anything that moved. All of her time spent training, she had never faced a situation where she was expecting to deal with two bigger men on the ground. One, she could handle. Get him in her legs and squeeze him unconscious, or trap his hands and knock him out.

Two was one too many. At least nobody had a gun in hand.

Yet.

She slid backwards away from another punch. Nobody had connected solidly with her yet, and the one she had been battering should be woozy from all the blows she had landed.

Rowena settled on her knees, as far away as she could get with one hand still gripping her jacket. It was almost like wrestling with an octopus, and she wasn't Japanese, so that wasn't a cultural kink she'd ever considered.

Instead, she broke that grip with an elbow and leaned into a punch. Not a lot she could put behind it like this, but she caught the man on the tip of the jaw and his eyes went glassy with concussion.

Just in time, too, because the first guard had finally wriggled more of less free, and he was trying to grab her. An improvement over finding a gun, because she'd lost track of two of them and the guy she'd just punched hadn't gotten his out, so it was still down in there somewhere.

Rowena braced her knees and let the man pull himself closer, using him like an anchor of some sort, even as he was trying to drag her down where his greater size and mass might give him an advantage.

She waited, arms tangled as they wrestled, then suddenly lunged forward and cracked her forehead into his face. She was seeing stars, but

Rowena had heard his teeth clack together and his eyes didn't look like they focused too well right now.

His grip loosened enough for her to punch him. Again. Again. An elbow. A backfist. Left hand free for a combination cross.

The guard collapsed.

Rowena felt like a horse that had just finished a mile and a quarter sprint, blowing like a *taifeng*, the dreaded winds that lashed Hong Kong regularly.

But she had no time. The elevator was descending. And the building was occupied. What would she do if the doors opened to a mob of more guards? Or even just salarymen wanting to go home

She rolled the nearest guard over and located his handcuffs, using them on the man while he was too woozy to resist. The second got the same treatment. She found her bag and hoped that she hadn't broken the laptop in the scuffle, but all she really needed was the hard drive if it came to that.

The guns got added to the collection she had amassed, though she kept her SIG. The silencer had cracked to the point of uselessness, so she threw it in the bag, quickly policing her mess, even as she watched the numbers descend.

At the last moment, she lunged out and hit the button for the second floor, rather than depositing her in the lobby with whatever else might be happening. Whoever might be waiting. She had no idea what had happened to Chace and her headset had stripped loose from the plug in the struggle.

She grabbed loose cables as the door opened and quickly made her way to the stairwell.

CHAPTER
THIRTY-NINE

Chase found himself alone in the hallway as the door closed suddenly.

Well, shit.

Idly, for about a half of an eyeblink, he considered hitting the button again, but had no idea who might be standing there when it opened, and didn't feel like holding someone at gunpoint to escape.

Or shooting everything that moved.

On the headphones, the sounds of struggle. Blows. Cries of pain. Bodies slamming into walls.

One Rowena against a pair of guards. He had no idea how good she was. Or how willing to shoot men whose only crime right how had been being hired to provide building security.

Not like the folks Chace was almost excited about dealing with. But not while he was holding a heavy lump of extremely stolen goods.

In the movies, this was always the moment when the hero had a backpack with a parachute in hit. Or a collapsible glider. Or friends with a helicopter who could swoop in and grab him off the roof.

Chace had his new shoes, a gun, and a lockpick. Not exactly a breakfast of champions kind of moment.

And if the guards had been summoned, more were coming.

He flipped a coin in his head and started for the nearest stairwell. Smart goons would send people up that way. Or at least keep watch.

Maybe he could get to the bottom before those Taiwanese caught on to Rowena's joke and got back here from wherever they'd been lured off to. A guy can dream, can't he?

Chace hit the firedoor at a jog, trying to find a comfortable way to hold this damned brick they'd gone to so much effort to steal. Then he had an idea.

Pausing, he put the thing down and stripped off the jacket, then wrapped the brick up in it and tied the sleeves into a knot he slipped over his head, carrying the weight like a baby on his belly. One hand held it kind of like an American football. He went ahead and drew the silenced SIG with the other and started down stairs.

The radio had gone dead, but that had happened in the middle of a fight, and he had no way to determine if Rowena had won or lost.

"Testing comm," he said simply.

"We read you," the man in the truck said. "Lost contact with number one."

"Understood," Chace said. "Stand by and keep watch."

He started down.

Twenty-three floors to go.

Rowena peeked out a firedoor and saw the lobby mostly empty. At least no guard at the station by the front door. Businessmen coming and going. Mostly going, heads down like they had been before.

No radio, as the wire had been pulled completely away from the plug and she needed to be outside in the darkness before she took the five minutes to disassemble it and try rewiring. Or digging in her bag and hoping she'd forgotten a spare with buds and a mic for her phone at some point.

She made a note to include spares when she built this new standard breaking-and-entering kit Chace had inspired.

Rowena ran her hands through her hair to make it less mussy, hoping that the black eye she could feel coming on wasn't too bad yet. She drew a breath and walked out the front door like she belonged here, drifting into the crowd of businessmen all headed somewhere to get drunk and hopefully make the pain and depression go away for a while.

Honestly, Russia and Japan had already peaked. China was right at the cusp. India crowded close behind.

Would she live through World War III, or watch all three collapse inwards instead of lashing out? Russia had already bitten off more than it could chew in Ukraine.

How bad were the next ten or fifty years going to get?

And what could she learn from Chace that might help, when things got really ugly? More and more, she wondered if the Americans would be the only survivors, safely isolated and hiding behind whatever paranoid defenses they'd built, possessing the world's most dangerous military machine.

Did she need to start moving more and more of their operations to the US, the so-called *Golden Mountain*? Again, was Chace the entry point that got them there safely, before everything else came apart?

Rowena found a coffee shop nearby. American chain trying to brute force Japan, and wealthy enough to sort of succeed, unlike Vietnam, who had extremely specific expectations about coffee.

She ordered a drink, then removed it to a corner and teased apart her headphone jack and the wire using a small knife she had remembered to include. Part of an electronics kit that needed to be rethought.

Nothing fancy needed here, she put the headphones on and used her thumbs to jump the raw wires into the gaps.

"One, testing," she said simply.

Static.

She tweaked a few things and tried again.

"Reading," her spotter replied. "Status and location?"

"Location four in ninety seconds," Rowena said. She could get everything organized and get there in that time. "Status of Two?"

"There's been a complication," Chace gasped.

CHAPTER
FORTY-ONE

Chace head a door open below him, before he was halfway to his destination on the ground.

Or hell, depending on who you asked.

Men, stomping up stairs quickly for now, because they had only just started a nasty stair climb.

Still, he didn't have long until he was face to face with whoever was coming for him.

Or in a firefight.

A quick inventory didn't leave him a lot of subtle options. Had they blown this one to the point that subtle was a wasted effort?

Chace hit the next floor and paused, moving to the exit door. Locked, but presumably a fire door that could be opened by pressing a bar on the other side.

Out came the snap gun and he jammed it into the lock, uncaring at this point if he destroyed the mechanism, as long as he could get it open.

Three jams and it surrendered. Possibly, something broken inside. Not his problem.

He pulled the door open looking like a burglar with a hand in the cookie jar, but there were no officers there to arrest him, so Chace slipped into the hallway and breathed.

Sticking his head back into the stairwell, it sounded like two or three men climbing. Slower now but deliberate, with that dull, slapping echo of shoes on metal steps.

Chace carefully put his bundle down and rooted in his pockets. He figured that he had a fifty/fifty chance who he was facing. And he needed to eliminate this group as a threat, because otherwise they might hear him once they got past or maybe look down and see him unless he moved slowly and carefully.

And the time for subtle had passed.

He left the bundle next to the door and listened. Definitely three men. Two in pretty good shape. One lagging a bit, but not much, as he kept ordering the other two to slow down and they listened without the good-natured grumbling of soldiers. So a squad leader and two goons.

Didn't sound like security guards, so he presumed that someone had notified the Dragon Scholar and he had either returned, or scrambled whoever was close to investigate when they couldn't reach the man they left behind.

Probably, that was it. A missed check in because the phone was in Rowena's bag. Hopefully, she had remembered to put it on airplane mode at some point before someone thought to track her with it, like they might have done him before.

So many little things that can trip you up in this game.

Rowena was suddenly on the line again.

"Location four in ninety seconds," her voice came through. "Status of Two?"

"There's been a complication," Chace replied quietly, hearing his own hoarseness from lugging that damned brick down fifteen flights of stairs and trying to be quiet. "Stand by for thirty seconds at my end."

If she'd said ninety, she was hopefully somewhere outside the building and had gotten through or around whatever cordon the goons were putting up. Hopefully, nobody had called the police yet, because he really didn't need to be arrested tonight while in possession of stolen goods.

Especially not these goods.

Yup, fuck subtle. Time to go junkyard dog, but not lethal. Hopefully.

Maybe.

If they got lucky.

Chace listened as the men got to the landing below him, pulling the door almost closed as he counted steps, breaths, and timing.

He pulled the pin on the flash-bang and softly let it roll through the gap, then pulled the door shut to protect his eyes and ears. One hand grabbed a bit of his jacket, the other was on the door handle.

BOOM!!!!!

Chace exploded into motion, drawing his little computer prize with him just enough that the cloth would keep the door from closing again. The world's weirdest and possibly most valuable door stop.

He'd caught the first two square with the flash and the bang of the grenade going off. Worse, contained in a small space with hard walls to reflect the sensory overload right back in your face.

No time to think, Chace shoved both stunned men over the railing, one bashing his skull on the next flight of stairs above before they fell about three meters, awkward, stunned, and unprepared.

Chace spun to the boss, who had been mostly facing the wrong direction to be looking, but was still blinking rapidly to clear his eyes and opening his mouth.

If he'd have known for certain that they were the bad guys, Chace might have just shot all three of them, but that was the luck of the draw.

Instead, he punched. The man had some training. Might even be pretty good normally, as his automatic reflexes brought up hand to block.

The original Chace Haig had studied Taiwanese Kung Fu and Okinawan Karate in the late 1950s and early '60s. The former was a softer form, emphasizing speed and flexibility, while the latter was often all about breaking boards and heads. Every Chace Haig since had learned the same curriculum, supplemented over the decades as Cantonese and Vietnamese folks brought their own styles and things merged in. Plus stuff other folks had invented or discovered.

The first block was automatic. The man was on automatic. Chace decided to overwhelm him and threw as many punches and kicks as he could. Plus a rude trick a parkour expert friend had taught him, where Chace turned and planted a foot on the nearby wall, exploding sideways with both hands to shove his foe.

Normally, not all that effective an attack.

Normally, the guy you pushed wasn't standing on the top step of a staircase.

He went over backwards when he tried to step back and found only air.

Two men below had only started to recover from falling when their boss landed atop them, with Chace in hot pursuit.

Subtle was past, but curb-stomping wasn't necessary. Instead, he grabbed heads and bonged them against steps and walls hard enough to concuss. Mixed with the after-effects of the flash-bang, they were unconscious quickly.

Chace ignored guns, collecting wallets and phones, then zip-tying his new friends with the last of his collection.

He paused, wondering how badly the building had echoed with some fool setting off explosives in a stairwell. Probably warned the folks above that something below was trouble.

Chace raced back to his door and found it open enough to grab the brick. He looked up and saw the fire alarm across the corridor.

He felt a look of utter rudeness take hold.

CHAPTER
FORTY-TWO

Rowena heard the sharp mindspike of the fire alarms start up down a block and across, and knew that Tokyo's citizens were about to lose their shit.

It was a cultural thing, in a place where buildings had been at risk of burning down and taking whole city blocks with them for centuries.

Much less likely today, but it was still buried in their psyche. Especially after what the Americans had done to them in the war.

Already, folks were pouring out of the target building in a panic, running for their lives with laptop computers, briefcases, anything important.

She got to the truck and heard the doors unlock as she moved closer. In and shut, they locked again.

"Status?" she asked the passenger.

"Two is supposedly inbound," he replied. "Fire alarms make communications impossible, but have also rendered our enemies at a disadvantage. We've spotted a couple of vehicles as probables, but police and fire rescue are vectoring down hard on this location. Orders?"

"Stay alert and watch for trouble," Rowena ordered, hearing the sirens bleat through the sides of the vehicle.

Anyone closer would be risking migraines.

More sirens wailed in the distance as truck companies converged. Pedestrians milled about, some drawing away while others were like moths seeing a light as they got pulled closer by unseen tides. At least the truck had a good spot. Not so close that they risked getting hemmed in by fire trucks, but not that far away, either.

"One, it's two," Chace suddenly said on the comm. "Location six."

"Location six," the driver replied instantly. "In motion. Forty seconds."

"Thirty would be better," Chace said, but fell to silence.

Rowena had somebody's pistol in hand as they moved. She wasn't sure which one she'd drawn from the bag, and there had been four in there. SIG, so probably hers. She honestly hadn't been paying that much attention at the time, rushing to get out of the building before more trouble arrived.

And Chace seemed to have made it as well.

They crossed a lateral intersection and Rowena spotted him moving out from a darkened doorway, still lugging that brick they'd gone to so much effort to steal.

But then, every man still in the building had probably grabbed something similar and ran, so Chace wouldn't have stood out that much in the process.

Was he that lucky or that good? And how soon would the two of them have to have a confrontation about whatever future they might have?

He was so much more than met the eye. At the same time, definitely not the man who had shot Father all those decades ago.

Could they find neutral ground?

The truck pulled to the curb and Rowena flung the door open as Chace got close. He handed her the deadweight and more or less fell into the back seat with her, pulling the door shut even as the driver was back in motion.

"Status?" he asked, a little breathless.

"I made it safe, after taking out the two guards," she said. "You?"

"Three KMT goons going up the stairwell," he nodded. "Flash-bangs are a bitch in a confined space. Not quite the old chunky salsa effect. Or at least nowhere but your brain. Left them all neutralized on six."

"Why the fire alarm?" she asked. "Doesn't that escalate the situation entirely out of control?"

"We were past subtle at that point," he nodded. "Flash-bangs going off where everyone inside would hear them. Unfortunately—for them at least—the first thing a fire alarm does is trigger every single elevator to immediately descend to the ground floor and lock itself down until someone with a key overrides it. I figured they were above me by then. At least the important folks. Trapping them there means they have to come down the same way I did. And the police will be asking questions if anyone starts looking at interior footage of what happened."

"Like, why the KMT has an office in that building?" Rowena grinned.

"Past tense," he laughed. "Somebody blew that cover and burned the place, so they have to start entirely over after this."

"And you didn't kill anybody?" Rowena pressed.

His grimace was telling.

"Like you, nameless, faceless minions," he replied. "At some point, I'll run into Dragon Scholar Zheng again and it won't be so polite."

Rowena couldn't help her flinch. Chace would have killed Zheng without any warning or provocation, even knowing that cameras would record it and her organization would know what happened, even if nobody else ever learned.

Who was Chace Haig? What was he?

"What now?" he asked, ceding operational authority to her, in spite of being a better trained agent. And a man.

She thrilled with the power he handed her, understanding what he was doing.

"Driver, drop us at our destination, then disappear to yours," Rowena called to the two men in front. "Han will be responsible for you until Hong Kong issues updated orders, but I expect you to have two to four days of downtime, so make the most of them but do so in hiding."

Grunts up front acknowledged. The KMT teams might have to flee in the dead of the night to escape Japanese police questions. Then they might decide to hit one of her facilities in retaliation.

The important ones had been cleared out, so nothing useful would come of such an attack, except further pissing off the locals at her enemies. She was a prepared as she could be.

Until she looked at Chace studying her and had to rethink that logic entirely.

Was anybody really ready for Chace?

Still, he smiled at her. She returned it.

One more battle ahead.

Chace focused on his breathing as the car drove across the Tokyo megaplex. An unknown location on the east side, according to what Rowena had told him, but he didn't really care that much.

He was committed.

Somewhere Dragon Scholar Zheng and that Kwok fellow would be screaming at each other and phones as the full impact of what he'd done became evident. Likely, they would find footage of him and Rowena and recognize them, so he had a new set of enemies.

All the more reason to get his ass out of Asia for a while.

Probably.

He caught her sidelong glances and understood that they had another conversation left to resolve. Chace could only hope that her father hadn't chosen to fly to Tokyo for it.

In that case, he'd be right proper fucked. Good thing he had a lot of ammunition on hand.

Then her hand slipped out and caught his, giving Chace a small squeeze that suggested maybe they didn't have to be mortal enemies.

Probably.

There was still a lot of thin ice between here and wherever. He wasn't looking forward to traversing it.

"Did you kill the phone you stole?" he asked her.

"Did," she nodded sagely. "Will also make sure that the laptop can't call for help when I open it, because I had a secured network at the far end and it would need 31-character passwords to access.”

Chace nodded back. That was about the limits of his understanding of computers, generally. Not the devices themselves, but how to keep them secured against intrusion and detection, because that was the underlying theme of his life.

They lapsed into silence at that point and rode through the darkness. More than once, Chace caught himself nodding off and jerked awake, angry with himself for almost losing control.

The mission wasn’t complete. Not yet. The raid might be, but he still had to face whatever she had set up at the far end.

Whoever.

The truck pulled to a curb and they were out quickly, her with her messenger bag, him with his bowling ball deadweight. No doorman, but she had a keycard that opened things, then got them onto a secured elevator.

Upstairs, the hallway was even better than the warehouse where Han worked. Expensive everything. Luxurious, even. A lot of money for a commons, but Chace supposed that folks up here paid a lot of money for the building.

He wondered if she owned it. Or her father did, through some impossible depth of holding companies. Old Hong Kong money was like that, from the bits and pieces he remembered. Invest on timelines measured in lifetimes, instead of quarters or years. Grow patiently and reap a massive windfall, if luck was on your side.

The hallway was empty. No night sounds at all, which was good. She led him down a hallway, then unlocked a door with a key and let him in.

Inside, a waiting room, for lack of a better term. Space to wait for someone important, without being in their space.

Quickly, she led him through a second door beyond, and Chace upped his estimate of her wealth another level. Floor to ceiling glass overlooking a balcony that wrapped a corner of the building and looked down on a river. He wasn’t sure which one, but big. Utterly stupendous view.

Lights were down, but she brought them up and he was impressed by the amount of available space. And the money spent decorating it. Living room alone was ten meters on a side, with a kitchen and dining space to one side, and a small library on the other. Then doors off.

"Do you need something to drink?" she asked, gesturing at a bar next to the kitchen.

"I need a shower," Chace admitted. "Stinky and sweaty."

"I know," she grinned. "Through here."

Hallway with doors to the side, and through the one on the end.

The master bedroom was larger than his apartment in Boston. And had closets and a bathroom off that. Hell, the bathroom was almost bigger than his apartment, when he got in there.

She'd tossed her bag on the bed as she went by. He'd put the brick on a dresser.

As he watched, she stripped off her jacket and dropped it on the floor.

"The shower is big enough for two," Rowena smiled. "Need someone to scrub your back?"

"I do," he smiled back at her.

And if she was in there with him, less chance that someone would pop out of a closet with guns.

Probably.

He got the new shoes off, then began stripping, pausing occasionally to admire her emerging from her clothes.

Muscles and curves.

"You know, last night about this time, we were headed for all sorts of trouble," Rowena observed, head cocked and a seductive grin on her face as he finished undressing. "And I remember something about a rain check."

"I need clean first," Chace countered, reaching out a hand and pulling the woman against his chest for a kiss.

A promise, as it were. Or something he got to keep if someone was about to jump them.

She returned it, then pulled him into the bathroom proper and got the showers running.

Two heads, at either end of a large space, with white tile underfoot and up the walls. Chace adjusted one of the handles cooler than she'd set it, but he'd never met a woman who didn't like her shower water too hot.

Not a lot of fooling around in the shower. Mostly ogling, because ogling. Lots of soap. Warm water that kept wanting to lull him to sleep.

Chace fought it off. Got dry and found a terrycloth robe to wrap around himself, even as she did the same.

"Now, I think I need a drink," he observed, taking her hand and drawing her to the bar.

Fully stocked. Exceptional selection. Top shelf labels.

He fixed himself a sidecar, because Chace Haig had always liked that drink. Cognac, orange liqueur, and freshly squeezed lemon juice, in this case with a rim of sugar to soften the bite.

"That looks good," she said as he finished, so Chace handed her the glass to sip. "Oh, yes."

He ended up making a second for himself.

"Now what?" he asked leadingly as they stood and sipped.

"There's a lot of work that needs to be done on those computers," she replied soberly. "They can wait until the morning."

Chace let her take his hand and draw him back into the bedroom, where the messenger bag got moved and he watched her drop the robe to the floor and smile at him.

"Let's go to bed," she announced.

Chace smiled and joined her.

If it was to be a last meal for the condemned, he intended to enjoy it.

CHAPTER
FORTY-FOUR

Rowena woke to the sun coming in through a curtain she'd forgotten to close. She was alone, when a hand reached out, and Chace's spot was cool to the touch.

She opened her eyes and sat up abruptly, looking around. Was he gone?

The bag and the NAS were still present, but she'd slept through Chace slipping out of bed at some point.

At least his shoes were still by the door. She grabbed her robe and put it on as she moved to the door.

Out in the main room, she found him doing karate kata in the open space. Not a form she's learned, but motions she recognized, though he was doing them softly and quietly. And wearing the slacks and shirt from his new outfit. Barefoot.

A glance in her direction and a smile, but he kept going, so Rowena shook her head and moved to the expensive coffee robot, grabbing a mug and telling it what to brew for her.

She got her coffee about the time he finished. She watched him as Chace moved nearby and fixed his own, the machine whirring and grinding enough that she supposed it would have awakened her.

Rowena didn't think of herself as a light sleeper, but Chace apparently moved like a ghost.

"How are you this morning?" he asked.

"I hurt in new places," Rowena admitted.

"The black eye doesn't help, I'm sure," he said.

She shrugged. Someone had connected during that wild scrum in the elevator. And she'd used muscles she hadn't in a long time, then and afterwards. It was a good hurt, though she might need to lay in a hot tub with bubbles at some point.

He moved to the refrigerator and pulled out various things. Continental style European breakfast, with cold cuts, cheeses, and a croissant that had been delivered for today.

"How soon will we know about our friends?" Chace asked, drawing her to the table and sitting across from her, stacked with munchies between that she nibbled on.

"I presume that they won't stop running for a few more hours," Rowena replied. "The Japanese government can't be pleased to have to deal with those folks two nights in a row. They'll have to vanish hard, then call Taipei to get them official cover."

Chace nodded, but didn't comment. How often was he in similar situations that he could acknowledge all that and move on, anyway?

"You told the driver two to four days," he noted. "Same for us?"

"Yes," Rowena agreed. "Maybe less, if the KMT people get chased out of Japan. Maybe longer if the Japanese decide to evict everyone and get messages to my people in Hong Kong."

"Whatever will we do to fill several days in isolation?" he asked her, eyes glittering with mischief. "The cupboards and freezer are full, so we don't need to go out for the night market."

"All part of the plan," she grinned. "Get you alone where I can test you."

They grinned. Last night, he'd obviously been exhausted, and still risen to the occasion, to the point she wasn't sure if she'd pulled a muscle in her stomach during an orgasm. All the more reason to soak later, if she was going to keep this routine up.

"Do you have the tools to crack those machines?" he asked. "We went through a lot of effort, and I'd like to know I stuck a really big finger in some asshole's eye over it."

Again, she was a bit surprised at the vehemence in his voice. He didn't ever sound like a spy. They tended to be extremely low profile and quiet folks, slipping away when nobody was looking.

Not going looking for trouble.

"After breakfast, I'll see what I can do immediately with the tools on hand," she assured him. "If the notebooks has the passwords to the laptop, it might be that the machine is configured to connect to the brick and see it as an open mounted drive."

"Meaning?"

"Meaning that it would be like plugging in a thumbnail to the side," she replied. "Nothing encrypted. Or I'd have the passwords to decrypt it on the fly. Steal everything."

"Sell it to the highest bidder?" he asked with a feral smile.

"I'm not sure who that might be," Rowena countered.

"I could make a few calls when you knew what you had," he said. "I'm sure the Taiwanese have a lot of enemies, assuming you don't have a number in Beijing you might ring up."

The casual way he said it jarred her. An obvious expectation that she was Chinese Intelligence. Somewhere. Something. When she wasn't.

Not really.

Fellow travelers, at best.

At best?

Did that describe Chace Haig? Patriotic enough when necessary, but out to make money for himself? If so, that was the opening she needed to get to his truth.

Whatever truth he might allow her to know.

Chace Haig was a closed book you had to estimate by the cover. It was a lovely cover, but there were deep secrets.

"I'm not planning to call Beijing," she decided. "At least not directly. If something leaks to them later, that's just their karma."

She paused and took a leap of...something. Faith? Risk? Rowena couldn't identify it easily.

"What about you?" she asked. "Who would you contact to buy such data?"

"Not my hemisphere, really," he shrugged. "Japanese might want to know what they were up to. Same with South Korea and Russia, or the US and the Five-Eyes. China's really their big enemy. Most likely to pay well for information about these folks. That's the currency I deal in. Not necessarily money, but certainly face and favors."

"Five-Eyes?" she asked, testing him.

"Intelligence structures for the US, UK, Canada, Australia, and New Zealand," he replied crisply. "Japan and Korea have hated each other for centuries, so they hardly share. Taiwan has to be quiet about things, so I hardly know how they operate, except that they feared you enough to send a hit team in broad daylight."

"Feared me?" she asked. "Me?"

"Nobody around here knows me, Rowena," he reminded her. "Or didn't. I expect a lot of folks are chasing down random leads and probably calling folks in London or Paris for tidbits. Most of the folks they'd find like me, however, so I should be safe enough."

Rowena let that go and chewed on a slice of meat.

"So what's next for Chace Haig?" she asked blithely. "Disappear at the airport, never to be seen again?"

She watched his eyes to see what lies he would spin.

Chace continued lifting the mug of coffee to his mouth and took a sip as he considered her words. Felt like a trap. Looked like one, however nice.

At some point, would she invite him to Hong Kong, however innocently it sounded, whereupon he just happened to meet the man he'd technically shot thirty-five years ago?

A jar better let undisturbed.

"I haven't killed anybody yet here," he offered as a distraction. "If that one guy dies or loses his leg, that's their failure of medical assistance, because it should have been a clean through-and-through with the ammunition they were using. At the same time, I can't imagine that they stop looking for me anytime soon. Best if I'm in a place where they stand out in a crowd more than I do. Puts them at a disadvantage, as it were. Especially since I'm hardly conversational in Japanese or Chinese. This was supposed to be a tourist vacation."

He watched her nod contemplatively.

"So I'd have to come to London or DC if I wanted a second date?" she asked, eyes giving nothing away.

"Or Zurich," he replied. "Technically, that's my home office, even if I don't spend a lot of time there. KMT folks will absolutely slam into a wall if they show up in Switzerland and get aggressive with the locals, for all the Swiss are extremely polite most of the time. What about you? Back to Hong Kong?"

"My home base," she nodded. "Likely a side trip to Beijing, as you noted, because they will want to know. I expect that they are reaching out to my people now to find out what happened, but that's us using overt force on a situation that is normally much more subtle."

"They started it," he reminded her. "I'd have happily let you have your way with me after dinner, then played other games, though I don't suppose either of us would have come to know as much detail about the other as we do."

She froze for a second, then relaxed. Chace couldn't help that he'd reacted the way he did. It had obviously kept them both alive when folks with guns came out of the crowd. And she knew who Chace Haig had been, once upon a time.

That knowledge had brought her to Tokyo. The last thirty-six hours had shown her more than she needed to know, but his options were starkly limited.

He could try to get recruited by this woman. He could walk away and burn things. He could end up killing her and having her father come after him wherever that man could hire killers.

Hell of a way to face a...Thursday morning.

"Why did you come looking for me?" Chace asked, willing to push right now.

He could burn this all down right now when they were alone and he might be able to get away. Certainly, the next Quartz call would be handled with an extra level of brutal ruthlessness, after those folks had been embarrassed once before.

Was it worth it?

She studied him. Measured her words. Lies? Maybe. Misdirections and mistruths, at least.

"Your name," she finally said, words clipped now.

"No relation to the former Secretary of State," he said, a fun way to distract people.

Alexander Haig had been a distant cousin of the original Chace and a loose contemporary, about a decade apart.

Her eyes crossed in confusion, which was his intent. Always cause interrogators to slide off the edge of their planning. They make mistakes or tell you more than they intended.

She blinked and cleared again a moment later.

"There was another Chace Haig," she said, confirming how thin the ice was under his feet. "Much older, obviously, because he and my father were enemies."

"When was this?" he asked, as innocently as he could sound.

"1988," she nodded. "When China was in the process of opening up under Deng, but before the first President Bush came to power and helped."

"Two years before I was born," he reminded her helpfully. "And Chace is an old English name. I'd be interested in finding out who he was. Whatever happened to the man?"

Chace knew, because he'd had to learn the history behind the name. The Second, taking the name from 1979 until 1993, after the original had been killed in Paraguay in '78. In a way, it was almost like that British science fiction show, where the actor got replaced every few years and they called it a regeneration.

Except that every Chace Haig had to look like the original. Act like him.

Be him.

"We don't know," Rowena admitted, so Chace knew he had some space to work with.

Or hide in later.

"Here in Japan?" he asked, further muddying the waters.

"No, Hong Kong," she said.

"I hardly know anything about Hong Kong, except that it used to be British, and the Chinese have been slowly cracking down hard on folks for the last twenty-some years," Chace acknowledged.

Although he could see a few deep dives when he got home. And a lot of reading. Part of the job.

"It is my home," Rowena said fiercely.

He nodded back.

Not his.

"Were you here to kill me?" he asked.

They were alone, save for whoever might be listening on microphones he hadn't been able to find this morning.

"I was sent to discover who you were," she countered.

Probably as honest an answer as he could expect, given the circumstances.

"And?" he prompted, wondering if they were about to go hand-to-hand right here over the table.

If they hadn't already.

"You are more than you seem," she stated bluntly.

"Gotta be dangerous, to run with the sorts of criminal lowlifes I interact with," he offered.

"There is that," she said. "And a spy would interact differently. Wouldn't go after other spies so readily. So dangerously."

"They started it," he growled. "I can't help if they thought they were the king shit. I'm hoping some idiot left a lot of valuable intelligence unencrypted data on that brick. Or the laptop. Something you can turn into a lot of money and power over those folks."

"And that," she said. "Again, spies act differently."

He shrugged.

That was EXACTLY why Chace Haig was a long-term, deepest-cover agent. A CIA/FBI/MI5/MI6 Joint Service Intelligence Strike Operation designed to infiltrate a single agent into the most dangerous places on Earth, and gain the contacts that his bosses needed in order to track really bad guys.

And occasionally kill them.

"I am a banker," he said, falling back on the topmost level. Mueller Investments of Zurich. Boutique and elite. "And, I suppose, a fence and a fixer, depending on how you look at things. Everything is entirely legal under Swiss law. That's all I care about."

She watched him. Chace placed every single object on the table, in case he needed to duck or strike. Her black eye made her look almost like a pirate in many ways. Puffy and angry, but strong and lethal.

Dangerously interesting woman.

"What would you do with the data on the computers?" she asked, sidestepping a lot of things.

Or assuming them and moving on to sharper questions.

"Nothing," he replied.

"Nothing?"

"Those are yours," he smiled. "I just helped you steal them. Fucking the local office of the KMT so badly they have to be extracted from Japanese jails is reward enough, as far as I'm concerned. Honestly, I could board a plane for Paris this afternoon if I thought I was safe. And didn't have other reasons to stay put."

"Oh?" she asked, brightening.

"Have you looking in a mirror lately?" he asked honestly. "I don't mean the eye, but the rest. Seriously amazing woman. Beautiful. Smart. Deadly. Capable. Sexy. Fun. Man would be dumb to walk away from that. Granted, I don't have much choice in the long term, because of what I do and who I do it for, but there's no reason to hurry, at least as far as I'm concerned. Don't know how you feel about being trapped in an apartment for several days with me."

He let that hang. Hopefully, he'd distracted her from really digging in and putting two and two together. At least today.

He could not be the Chace Haig who shot Yan-Li Cai. Absolutely.

But they were in the same business. And it didn't take much to wonder which business that was.

As long as he stayed out of Hong Kong until he knew what was awaiting him there.

Or who.

Still, she smiled wryly. Sideways, like a woman used to hearing those compliments, but not believing them most of the time.

Most of the time.

This wasn't a woman you burned and merely walked away from. You'd better be running.

More likely, she'd tire of you and toss you out on your ass.

But for a few days, maybe he could actually have something of a vacation, if they were careful.

He'd come to Japan to escape work for a bit, though it had followed him.

"I might like that," she said carefully.

"Might?" he asked, mock-indignant and sarcastic.

"You'll probably have to work pretty hard at it to convince me," she smiled wider now.

Chace stood up and leaned across the table to kiss her, because she seemed to be inviting it.

"Mistress, challenge accepted," he said.

EPILOGUE

Chace sat across from Thane and waited for her to finish reviewing some folder filled with pages.

Finally, she closed it, dropped on on a pile in front of her, and looked up at him.

They were in her office in Zurich. Almost official-looking because he expected any number of people were looking closer at his legend right now.

Might as well lean hard into it.

"I would say you are the luckiest man alive," she began, "but that was one of the reasons I selected you for this job in the first place. That intuition."

Chace shrugged, unwilling to deny it.

He called it the Night Sounds. Those whispers—possibly in the back of his head—that had kept him alive more than once.

Especially over the last month or so.

"And she fell for it?" Thane pressed.

"I gave her enough to put the pieces together," he countered. "But they were the wrong pieces. Misdirection and obfuscation, while setting myself up to have the KMT and maybe all of Taiwan's Intelligence apparatus pissed at me, so I'd appreciate if you put out fingers to make sure they weren't hiring German assassins in the near future."

"Did that as soon as you shot that one boy," she grinned. "He's entirely burned and will be on a desk job for the rest of his career, but I'm told won't even have a limp in six months. And those three in the stairwell all recovered fine after they got tossed out by the Japanese government. Would you have killed them?"

"Maybe," he replied. "No easy way to handle that sort of situation halfway, but right up until I made positive identification, it was possible that they were more security guards or Tokyo cops, and none of those people were on my list."

"You are officially on theirs, so stay out of Taiwan," Thane told him. "I've talked with some people and there are a lot of extra resources being dumped into that field of operations over the next few years. If you stay off their radar, you should be safe."

"If," he nodded.

"Yes, if," she agreed. "I've read your debrief on Rowena Cai. I disagree that you might be able to recruit her into anything useful, but I will grant you that you've left yourself an opening you can exploit to penetrate her organization."

He grinned at her choice of words. Her grin told him that they hadn't been accidental. Certainly, four days in an apartment with the woman had been marvelous.

And they'd talked, too.

"I'm the guy you call when you have a need," Chace said with a negligent shrug. "I'll find you the guy you need to talk to. Her people are watching the way Beijing is ramping up a lot of trouble with Taipei, and want to make sure that they have some cover when the shit finally does hit the fan and everyone decides to crush China militarily. The PRC makes a lot of noise about sovereignty and historical legacies, but they don't really understand how much the US and its various allies hate the Party."

Thane nodded.

"You have an arc running clockwise from Seoul to Canberra," she agreed. "Plus the Philippines and Vietnam, among others, all of whom have gotten tired of Chinese braggadocio over the South China Sea. That war, if it comes, will be ugly."

"And everyone is taking the lessons of Ukraine and upgrading their kit and tactics accordingly," Chace said. "I read something on my flight home about secret Taiwanese cruise missiles that could hit the Chinese mainland at significant distances. Also, other missiles that might be able to hit Beijing?"

"I haven't asked to be briefed on that material yet," she shook her head. "Assume it is about half truth and half bluff to keep everyone honest. What is Cai going to want?"

"I got the impression that they own and operate a whole bunch of cargo ships, both hauling raw materials inward to Chinese ports as well as containers out," he said. "If and when I hear from her next, I expect her to ask for an introduction that gets her into London, Rotterdam, or American ports with goods. And all the usual smuggling, but if we know who's doing it, I presume that you'll be to forward useful tidbits to law enforcement."

"And track the buyers down and take them out," Thane nodded. "But that's tomorrow's operation. I had promised you a vacation from duty, so as far as I'm concerned, we can keep answering your email and texting people tidbits for another few weeks. What do you need?"

Chace smiled at her. When he'd taken the job, this older black woman had come across as gruff and mean. Tougher than everyone else in the building, because she'd been one of the first black women hired when the FBI allowed them to start carrying guns in the field.

Somehow, she'd also turned into something of a mother figure. Or confessor.

A lot of what he needed, given the monasticism of his chosen life.

"I plan on catching a train to Nice first thing tomorrow morning," he replied. "Then maybe laying on the beach a bit. Possibly a day trip to Monaco, depending on my company."

"Oh?" Thane asked, perking up.

"Rowena Cai promised to fly in tomorrow," he smiled. "Something about seeing my world, after being deeply immersed in hers for a madcap week."

"As long as you think it's safe," Thane said, sobering. "Obviously, there will be folks watching."

"And hopefully, those extra watchers will make me safe, because smart spies will avoid the area like a plague, while dumb criminals might have to walk up and say hello," he nodded. "And I can introduce her on to a whole new cast of villains for you to track and bust at some point."

"You stay safe," she enjoined him sharply. "I don't care what she does, but I've got plans for you."

"This is a working vacation, boss," Chace nodded. "Nothing more. I'll be on duty twenty-four-seven."

"Uh huh," Thane replied with a grunt.

"After all, how much trouble can I get into in France?" he asked.

"That's what worries me."

READ MORE

To read more of my fiction, sign up for my newsletter. You'll also get a free book!

http://www.blazeward.com/newsletter/

ABOUT THE AUTHOR

Blaze Ward is a prolific Indie writer and publisher who works mostly in Science Fiction and Light Thriller, with occasional forays into lots of other genres like superheroic fantasy.

You can find more of his titles at www.blazeward.com/books, www.KnottedRoadPress.com and wherever else you buy your books.

He also edits Boundary Shock Quarterly, an SF magazine he founded in 2018, and Thrill Ride Magazine.

ABOUT KNOTTED ROAD PRESS

Knotted Road Press publishes dynamic fiction set in exotic locations. Our authors cover a wide range of genres including science fiction, fantasy, mystery, literary, and poetry. We also have unique non-fiction voices in genres such as autobiography, business, cookbooks, and how-tos. We offer both DRM-free ebooks and print books for a global readership.

www.KnottedRoadPress.com

www.ingramcontent.com/pod-product-compliance
Lightning Source LLC
Chambersburg PA
CBHW070537100726
47907CB00004B/1150